The Old West F

VAN HOLT

THE
RETURN OF
FRANK GRABEN

Ride the Old West

Cover and Book design: KB Graphix & Design • www.kbdesign1.com
First Printing, 2013. Printed in the United States of America.

CHAPTER 1

Molly Wilkins saw him shortly after sunrise that morning, sitting his blue roan on the barren rocky slope above the Wilkins shack. A tall man in black, with a bleak weathered face and cold gray eyes narrowed to glittering slits.

The girl ran screaming to the shack. "He's come back! It's Frank Graben! He's come back!"

Her fat stolid mother was cooking breakfast at the fireplace. "Hush, girl. Don't talk nonsense. Frank Graben is dead."

"It's him, I tell you!" the excited girl cried. "Look up there on that ridge!"

Mrs. Wilkins looked out the window. "There's no one up there. You only thought you saw someone. Now wash your hands and help me get breakfast ready."

Homer Wilkins sat up on the plank bed, yawning and rubbing his eyes. "What's all the fuss about? Can't a man get no sleep around here?"

His wife shot him a hard look. "It's time you was up and doin' anyway, Homer Wilkins. What's to become of us the good Lord only knows."

Homer Wilkins sat on the edge of the bed in his patched overalls and faded red underwear. "Now don't you set in on me again, Hettie," he said placidly, while he contemplated a big toe that protruded from a hole in his sock. "You know how my back hurts from sleepin' on that hard bed."

"Pa, I saw Frank Graben up on the ridge," Molly said.

"Hush, girl," Mrs. Wilkins said. "You know Frank Graben is dead."

"I tell you it was him!" the girl insisted. "Or his ghost!"

"Don't talk foolishness. I've told you time and again—"

"Hold on, Hettie," Wilkins said, and looked at his daughter. "We don't know for a fact he's dead. Ain't nobody seen his body. The man you saw, Molly—what kind of horse was he ridin'?"

"That blue roan! And it was Frank Graben! I know it was him!"

"I didn't see anyone," Mrs. Wilkins said. "Molly's got too much imagination, like I've said before."

"Well, there's only one way to find out," Homer Wilkins said, pulling on his boots. "I'm goin' to town."

"Any excuse not to do no work around here," Mrs. Wilkins said bitterly.

It was midmorning when Frank Graben rode down Hackamore's short dusty street, which at this hour was deserted. The whole town looked deserted. He studied the frame and adobe buildings with sharp gray eyes as he rode past. At the lower end of the street he reined in before the livery stable. As he swung down a stout, potbellied man came out and watched him with silent hostility.

Graben gave the man a cold glance. "You don't seem too surprised to see me."

"I figgered you'd be back," Barney Ludlow said in a harsh, bitter tone. "It ain't easy to kill a disease."

"You better keep that in mind," Graben said as he slung his saddlebags and blanket roll over his shoulder.

"Don't think it's over," Ludlow warned him. "You can't kill a man like Whitey Barlow and get away with it. The Star hands will be comin' after you with a rope."

"They'll need more than a rope," Frank Graben said in a quiet, grim tone, and walked up the street to the hotel.

The man behind the desk had seen him ride past the hotel and had time to compose himself. Yet his pale face glistened with sweat, and reminded Graben of a tree from which the bark had just been stripped. Sam Dauber kept his eyes lowered and remained silent as he pushed the register toward the tall man in black and watched him sign his name.

Graben laid the pen down and glanced at Dauber's sweaty face.

"Things have sure changed," he observed, with his dark brows slightly raised and his gray eyes still narrowed to cold slits.

Dauber still did not say anything and did not look at him. He just handed Graben a key with the room number written on the attached tag.

Graben carried his blanket roll and saddlebags up to his room on the second floor. It was the same room he had had before, overlooking the narrow street. There was an iron bedstead with a lumpy mattress and clean sheets, a bureau with a mirror, a chest of drawers with a pitcher of water and a basin on top. Graben lowered his stuff to the floor, glanced through the window at the street, then took off his hat and washed his face and hands. Drying on a threadbare towel, he glanced at himself in the mirror and sighed.

He was not quite twenty-eight, but his bleak weathered face looked closer to thirty-five. There were permanent squint wrinkles around the hooded gray eyes—eyes so cold that few people could meet them without flinching. It would still have been a remarkably handsome face if he had smiled. But he never did, except in a wry, mocking way. The hair alone did not displease him. It was dark brown hair with a slight wave and reddish-copper glints.

He knocked the dust from his flat-crowned black hat and put it back on. Then he drew the double-action .41 Colt from his waistband, spun the cylinder and checked the loads. Tucking the gun back in his waistband, he opened the door and went down the stairs, a tall lean man, as graceful on his feet as he was in the saddle.

He gave Sam Dauber a narrow glance as he passed the desk but Dauber was careful not to look at him, lest Graben see the dislike and resentment in his dull eyes. Outside, Graben tramped along the boardwalk and pushed in through the swing doors of the Last Chance Saloon. There was no one in the saloon except for the man behind the bar. Without waiting to be asked, the man set out a bottle and a glass. His face had the same wooden expression, the same look of dull hostility and resentment Graben had seen on the faces of Sam Dauber and Barney Ludlow.

Graben poured himself a drink, lit a thin black cigar and looked at the saloonkeeper through slitted eyes. "Things have sure changed," he said.

Max Rumford slowly raised his bloodshot eyes and looked at Graben with hatred. He looked like a red-eyed bull getting set to charge, but he only said softly, "Maybe not as much as you think."

A horse trotted long the street, saddle leather creaked and a moment later a swarthy man with a dirty brown mustache pushed in through the batwing doors. His sleepy dark eyes widened in surprise when he saw Graben. Then the mustache curved away from yellow teeth in a cheerful grin. "Hello, Frank," Lum Mulock said as he stepped up to the bar. "I heard you was dead."

"Oh?" Graben said coolly. "Where did you hear that?"

Mulock grinned and scratched his dimpled chin. "I heard it somewheres." He glanced at the birdshead Colt in Graben's waistband. "Where are them Russian pistols you had, Frank?"

"As you may recall, I hardly ever wear them."

Mulock was grinning at him out of the corners of his eyes. "Seems like I saw somebody else wearin' them."

"If you see him wearing them again," Graben said, "tell him to get ready."

"Ready for what?"

"A hotter climate," Graben said.

Lum Mulock's eyes brightened with interest. He tasted his drink and smacked his lips with relish. "Rube and the boys will be real pleased to hear you're back," he said. "Things have been a lot more peaceful around here since you killed Whitey Barlow."

"Except for one thing," Graben said. "I didn't kill him."

"That a fact?" Mulock's grin got even broader, showing his meaty red lips as well as his crooked yellow teeth. "Wonder why ever'body around here thinks it was you."

"I guess somebody put the idea in their heads," Graben said, watching Mulock with cold narrow eyes.

Mulock wiped his mouth with the back of a dirty brown hand. "It was a easy idea for them to believe," he said. "Ever'body knows how you and old Whitey hated each other at first sight."

That, Graben had to admit, was not so far from the truth, and he found himself thinking about that cold windy day five months before when he had first seen Whitey Barlow.

Graben had stopped at a waterhole in what seemed to him the middle of nowhere, over near the eastern edge of that vast desert plain surrounded by barren gray mountains. It had been days since he had passed a town or even a house, and he had not known there was a ranch anywhere around, although there were some old cow tracks near the waterhole. Then the five riders had come up out of an arroyo two hundred yards away and cantered toward him in a cloud of dust. They must have spotted him at a distance and waited for him in the arroyo, or he would have seen them or their dust earlier. That thought made him uneasy and he was not reassured by the rapid, businesslike manner of their approach.

Yet he took his time about filling his canteen and hanging it back on the saddle horn. Then he stood beside his horse and his slitted gray eyes watched the group as they charged up and halted, looking them over with a cool reserve.

The man in the lead was a white-haired man in his late forties or early fifties, a tall gaunt man with icy blue eyes and a face tanned to old leather. The rider beside him was just as tall, and more strongly built. He had dark eyes and a strong face covered with black beard, and he was a good twenty years younger than the white-haired man.

It was the white-haired man who asked in a sharp, rude tone, "What are you doing here?"

"Watering my horse," Graben said.

"This is my water," the white-haired man said. "Move along."

Graben did not like the man's tone or his manner. "This your land?" he asked.

The white-haired man blinked once, as if surprised by the question. There was the slightest hesitation before he replied. "As far as you're concerned, it is."

"Not good enough," Graben said. "Unless you can show me a deed to this land, you can go to hell."

The black-bearded fellow's dark eyes hardened with a look of anger. "Mister, this here's Star range," he snapped.

"I'll do the talking, Graf," Whitey Barlow said, his eyes still on Graben. "You've got a lot to learn about this country, mister."

"I know all about this country," Graben said flatly as he stepped into the saddle, never taking his narrow eyes off the five men. "And I know all about men like you. You probably don't even own the ground you roost on, yet you think you've got some God-given right to all the range you may ever want or need and nobody else can ride across it without your permission. Well, I'll repeat what I said a minute ago. You can go to hell." He deliberately ran his cool eyes over all five of them and added, "You can all go to hell for all I care."

Graf's chest tightened with anger, and his hand started toward his gun.

"If you touch that gun I'll kill you," Graben said in a soft, deadly tone. "And then I'll kill Whitey."

"Hold it, Graf," Whitey said harshly, his pale eyes glowing with anger. "I know how to handle men like him." Then he spoke directly to Graben. "Mister, I advise you to turn around and head back the way you came. What lies between these mountains is all Star range, and you won't find no welcome in my town. I'll make sure of that."

"Oh, you own the town too?" Graben said dryly.

After a moment the man slowly nodded. "You'll think I do, if you try to go there. You'll think I own the town and everybody in it."

With that he reined his horse around and rode back the way he had come, and Graf and the others reluctantly followed, looking back over their shoulders at Graben.

Watching them ride off, Graben had seriously considered following Whitey Barlow's advice and heading back over the mountains the way he had come. He knew that would be the smart thing to do. But there was nothing back that way worth going back to, and it was not in him to run from trouble.

After about a minute he had ridden on in exactly the same direction he had intended to go all along, which was almost in the same direction that the Star men had gone. And as he walked and trotted his horse out across that mountain-rimmed desert plain, he watched those five men draw slowly away from him, heading northwest. But after a while one of them left the others and headed straight west, and somehow Frank Graben knew that one was on his way to the town Whitey had mentioned.

On the outskirts of the town, several hours later, Graben met the rider heading back the way he had come. They met and passed without speaking, the Star hand scowling darkly, Graben watching him with cool eyes, deliberately turning his head to watch the man ride off and to let him know he did not trust him behind his back—a deliberate insult that was not missed by the Star hand glaring around to watch him also.

Then the blue roan was walking along the dusty street, and Graben turned his attention to the silent, deserted-looking town. When he reined in before the stable and started to dismount, Barney Ludlow came out, looked him over with hard eyes and spoke in a harsh flat tone that might have been borrowed from Whitey Barlow himself.

"Keep moving. I don't want your business."

Graben relaxed in the saddle and watched the short, potbellied man in silence for a moment. Then he asked, "Do you own this place, or does that rancher?"

Barney Ludlow's eyes were mean, his voice as harsh as before. "Whitey Barlow is a good friend of mine," he said. "If it wasn't for the Star Ranch there wouldn't be a town here. And you'll find everybody in Hackamore feels the same way I do."

After a moment Graben silently turned his horse and rode back along the street to see if that was true. At the only restaurant he reined in, dismounted, tied his horse and went inside. Behind the counter stood a gray-haired woman with a wrinkled face who might have been Whitey Barlow's sister. Graben sat down at a table and said, "Get anything to eat around here?"

She looked at him with hard eyes and asked, "You the one had that run-in with Whitey Barlow?"

Graben silently nodded, his eyes cold.

"Then you better keep moving," the woman said. "We don't want your kind around here."

Graben thought about that for a moment. "My kind?"

"You know what I mean," the woman said, looking out the window at the empty street as if she expected to see Whitey Barlow and his men riding into town.

"I'm not sure I do," Graben said. "Maybe you'd better tell me."

The woman looked at him with scorn. Then, without another words, she went into the kitchen in back and slammed the door. Graben sat there for a few minutes, but somehow he knew that he could wait there forever and the woman would not come back out until he left. So he got up and went back out to his horse. He untied the horse and led him across the dusty street to the hotel, while Sam Dauber watched apprehensively through the window. The hotel man's face was drenched with sweat by the time Graben opened the door and entered the lobby.

Dauber was already shaking his head, a scared but stubborn look in his eyes, as Graben approached the desk. "I'm sorry, mister," he said in an unsteady voice, "but we ain't got no rooms for rent."

Showing no surprise, Graben thumbed his hat back on his head. "What about something to eat, then?" he asked.

Again the man shook his head, almost desperately. He took out a handkerchief and mopped his face. "It's too late for lunch and we don't serve supper till six." He fumbled for his watch and looked at it. "That's nearly four hours from now."

"I guess I'll just have to come back then," Graben said dryly.

"It won't do no good," Dauber said. "We only serve our guests and regulars who eat here all the time. It's a hotel policy."

For a time Graben regarded the man in silence, and Dauber could not meet his cold gray eyes. Then Graben turned away and went out to the veranda and sat down in one of the chairs, his weathered face blank as he looked along the deserted street. He was trying to decide what to do.

For some time now there had been a feeling in his gut that he was going to die. He did not know how or when, but instead of going away as expected, the feeling had got worse until he could no longer ignore it. He had started being more careful, had even gone out of his way on several occasions to avoid trouble. And he had come here, to this remote place, looking for peace. Instead of finding it, he had just found more trouble.

He knew what he should do. He should ride on. He also knew he would not do it. Not now. He couldn't, being the kind of man he was. Whitey Barlow and the people of this town had made that impossible.

He glanced at the blue roan standing at the rail. Though tired from long travel, the gelding had his head raised, his bright dark eyes watching Graben expectantly. When Graben left the horse tied at a hitchrail it usually meant that he would be riding on in a few minutes. Otherwise he would put the horse in the nearest stable or corral and see that he was properly cared for.

Graben got to his feet, stepped off the porch, untied the horse and led him down the street to the Last Chance Saloon.

The red-faced, heavyset bartender with gray hair curling about his ears watched through bloodshot eyes as Graben came in through the swing doors.

Graben dug a coin out of his pocket and laid it on the bar. "Whiskey," he said.

The saloonkeeper smiled a tiny humorless smile. "Fresh out," he said.

Graben glanced at the bottles lined up on the back bar. Then, silently, he drew the birdshead Colt from his waistband and placed it on the bar near the saloonkeeper.

Max Rumford's bloodshot eyes rested on the gun for a long moment. "That thing supposed to scare me?" he asked.

"Did I hear you say you were fresh out of whiskey?"

Rumford nodded. "That's right."

"Well, if you ain't you soon will be," Graben said quietly, and lifting the gun he calmly and unhurriedly shattered four of the full bottles on the back bar. Then, while the whiskey still ran off the back bar and dripped to the floor, he looked at the red-eyed saloonkeeper and said, "One left."

Rumford did not move for a long moment. It seemed that he had even quit breathing. The bloodshot eyes watched Graben with hatred. Then he slowly took a bottle and a glass from the back bar and poured Graben a drink. He silently watched him drink the whiskey and made no move to pick up the coin.

Leaving the coin on the bar, Graben thrust his gun back into his waistband and said, "You can charge the damage to Whitey Barlow." Then he went out and Rumford's bloodshot eyes followed him like red bullets.

CHAPTER 2

Graben led the blue roan down the street to the livery stable. Barney Ludlow marched out and said flatly, "Mister, I told you to keep moving. I don't want your business."

Graben saw the anger in the man's bulldog face. He glanced at Ludlow's potbelly and felt a momentary desire to sink his fist into it. But like most gunfighters he usually avoided fistfights. A man with a stiff swollen hand could get himself killed if he needed to use a gun in a hurry. In any case, fistfights were virtually unheard of in a land where people settled their differences with guns.

"How'd you like a bullet in that fat gut?" he asked.

Barney Ludlow's face went slack with surprise. A look of caution replaced the anger in his eyes. "You'd shoot a unarmed man?"

"I never have before," Graben said. "But I might make an exception in your case. I'm seriously thinking about it."

Barney Ludlow drew a deep breath. His fists were clenched and his voice shook with anger. "I ain't no gunfighter," he said. "And there ain't no law here to deal with men like you. But you ain't gonna make no friends in this town the way you're going, I can tell you that. Why don't you do yourself a favor and ride on. We don't want your kind around here."

It seemed to Frank Graben that he had heard that before. His narrow eyes glittered like ice. "What kind is that?" he asked.

"The kind that threatens to shoot unarmed men," Barney Ludlow said bitterly.

Graben bared strong white teeth in a wolfish grin. "Just between ourselves," he said in a low, confiding tone, "it wouldn't do you any good if you were packing a gun. You wouldn't stand a chance."

His nonchalant, arrogant manner was more insulting to Barney Ludlow than his words. But the angry stable keeper merely watched in silence as Graben untied his blanket roll and saddlebags from behind the cantle and slung them over his left shoulder.

Then Graben, no longer smiling, looked at him through those cold, narrow eyes and said quietly, "Don't take it out on my horse. I might not like it."

Barney Ludlow's face turned red with resentment. "I never intended to. I happen to like horses. Which is more than I can say for some people."

"Then we have one thing in common," Graben said in an indifferent tone, and walked back along the street to the hotel.

Sam Dauber stood behind the desk, pale and trembling, when Graben entered the lobby with his saddlebags and blanket roll. There was a wild look in Dauber's eyes and he opened his mouth to say something. But just then a woman of about forty, still slender and attractive despite a few lines in her face, suddenly appeared from nowhere and touched Dauber's arm and murmured something. Dauber's mouth closed and his eyes watched Graben with silent hatred. It was the woman who turned the register around and laid a key beside it. Then she stood quietly beside her husband with her eyes lowered and her pale lips pressed together while Graben, after one cool glance at them, picked up the pen and wordlessly signed his name. That was how he checked into the Hackamore Hotel.

In his room overlooking the street, he reloaded the birdshead Colt and laid it on the bed. Then he washed up and put on a clean blue shirt and a pair of dark gray trousers from his saddlebags. He rarely wore the double-breasted blue shirt or the dark gray trousers. Usually he wore the dusty black shirt, also double-breasted, and the black trousers he had taken off. He had two corduroy jackets, one brown, the other black. The black one was close-fitting, unlined, and only reached to his belt. He had two black bandanna handkerchiefs and always wore one of them knotted loosely about his neck.

From his saddlebag he removed a black leather shell belt and two holstered revolvers, Smith & Wesson .44 Russians. The gun on the left was in a cross-draw holster with the butt turned to the right. If need be Graben could shoot all right with his left hand, but it was a rare occasion when he needed to. He cleaned the two pistols and after a moment's hesitation he put them and the shell belt back in the saddlebag. Then he stretched out on top of the bed with his hands clasped behind his head.

The bed was soft, but not too soft, and he should have found it mighty comfortable after weeks of sleeping on the ground. Yet he could not relax. His thoughts went back to the bleak rocky farm in Missouri where he had grown up. His father had lost an arm at Gettysburg and had never done any work after that. He spent most of his time in town, in the saloons, talking about the war. Frank and his brother Tom, two years older, had done all the work on the farm and in the winter they had hired out and cut and hauled firewood for people.

The two boys were almost always together and that should have made them feel close to each other, and in some ways it had. Yet they had never been able to get along. If they were not arguing there was a bitter silence between them. Most of the things they had argued about made no sense now, and Frank suspected that more often than not it had been his fault. Tom, being older, had naturally wanted to take the lead, but Frank had not wanted to follow, and had resented it when Tom tried to tell him what to do.

After their parents died they had sold the farm to pay off their father's debts, and then they had gone their separate ways. That had been over ten years ago and Frank had not seen Tom since or heard from him. He did not know if his brother was alive or dead. If Tom was still alive, he probably would never hear about it if Frank himself was killed. It gave Frank a lonely, empty feeling to think about it—a feeling that soon deepened into bitterness. The thought of dying did not bother him near as much as the thought that if he was killed the men who did it would be alive after he was dead. He could not bear the thought of them laughing and talking and enjoying the clean fresh air and sunshine while Frank himself fed the worms or the buzzards.

A man never remembers going to sleep, and when he woke up, late in the afternoon, Graben could not remember getting sleepy. But he remembered the feeling of bitterness, because the bitterness and the lost empty feeling were still there. That was the first thing he was conscious of on awaking, that hollow feeling in his gut, even before he noticed the dimness of evening creeping into the room.

He swung his feet to the floor and sat up on the edge of the bed, running his fingers back through his hair, thinking that it must be getting on toward suppertime. It was only then that he remembered what a hostile town this was, and how little chance there would be of getting a meal without the threat, voiced or implied, of violence.

He reached for his saddlebags and started to drag out the shell belt and holstered Russians. But again he changed his mind and shoved the heavy guns back. He was more comfortable without them, especially when sitting down, and he did not expect any serious trouble yet—nothing he could not handle with the light birdshead Colt, which he tucked into his waistband before leaving the room and going down the stairs.

Sam Dauber was not at the desk, and there was no one in the dining room when Graben entered. He sat down at a table with his back against the wall where he could watch the room and the street through the window without turning his head.

Almost as soon as he was seated, the slender, graceful woman he had seen earlier at the desk came through a door at the back and crossed the floor with a faint rustle of skirts. He noticed that there was a little gray in her dark hair, but he decided that she might be a little younger than he had thought at first, perhaps no more than thirty-seven or thirty-eight. In the yellow lamplight her eyes were a greenish hazel. She gave him a brief worried glance and then asked softly, "What would you like?"

"What have you got?"

"Roast beef, beans and potatoes. Apple pie for dessert."

"That sounds fine," he said in a gentler tone. "And some black coffee, please."

She seemed surprised at the "please," and gave him a wondering look. She seemed on the point of saying something, but then changed her mind and went back into the kitchen.

A group of riders entered town and trotted down the street, the hoofs of their horses muffled in the thick dust. Graben glanced through the window but by then the street was too dark for him to make them out. One turned in at the hotel rack. The others went on to the saloon. Graben heard the street door open and close. A moment later a tall slender young woman with dark hair and green eyes entered the dining room and stopped in her tracks when she saw Graben. He was struck by her beauty, but puzzled by the way she stood there and watched him with a catlike glow in her eyes. It was not at all a friendly look.

Then the Dauber woman came in from the kitchen with a tray, and the younger woman turned her back to Graben and he heard her ask softly, "What's that man doing here?"

Mrs. Dauber shook her head silently, a tight stricken look on her face. She brought the tray on to Graben's table, set it down without looking at him, then went quickly back across the floor, took the younger woman by the hand and led her into the kitchen. Graben could hear them talking in low tones but could not tell what they said.

He turned his attention to his food, but had barely begun eating when Whitey Barlow appeared at the door to the lobby and stared at him with a cold gleam in his pale blue eyes. "Mister," the rancher said in the blunt voice Graben did not like, "I thought I told you to keep moving."

Without a word, Graben laid the birdshead Colt on the table beside his plate and kept eating, trying to ignore the man until he could finish his meal. He hoped Barlow would take the hint and go away.

But Whitey Barlow was not a man to be scared away so easily and he was certainly not one to be ignored. He looked at the gun on the table and asked, "What good will that toy do you? This here's a .45 on my hip. Even if you shoot me with that thing, I can still kill you before I die. And if I don't, my men will. They should be here any minute now."

Mrs. Dauber and the dark-haired young woman stepped into the room from the kitchen and stood there near the door, silently watching.

"You women get back in the kitchen," Whitey Barlow said harshly.

"This is our hotel, Whitey Barlow!" Mrs. Dauber said, visibly shaken and sounding a little shrill. "And there's not going to be any trouble here." She suddenly raised her voice. "Sam!"

Whitey Barlow's voice was as ruthless as before, and now it was also edged with sarcasm. "Sam's at the saloon, getting drunk and talking himself into throwing this fellow out personally. If you don't aim to have no trouble here, you better talk to your husband first."

"Oh no," Mrs. Dauber said softly, wringing her hands.

The dark-haired girl had her accusing green eyes on Frank Graben, blaming him for their predicament. "Why don't you just go? That would solve everything."

He gave her a chilly glance from under his dark brows, but said nothing. He knew that if he offended a woman, whether intentionally or unintentionally, everyone in this town would feel honor-bound to defend her.

"Kate," Whitey Barlow said in a stern voice that would brook no opposition, "I told you to stay out of this. One more word from you and I'll send you back to the ranch."

Glancing at the girl in surprise, Graben saw her face redden and her thin lips tighten with resentment, but she remained silent. Apparently she was Barlow's daughter, and Graben slowly digested this fact with his food. It was not so easy to swallow. He would have guessed that if she was related to anyone around here it was the Dauber woman. She in no way resembled Whitey Barlow—unless it was in her arrogant manner.

Barlow had turned his pale gleaming eyes back to Graben. His mouth was open to speak, but at that moment another group of riders entered town, and the shuffling and snorting of the horses and the reckless laughter of the riders themselves distracted the rancher's attention. He shifted uneasily in the doorway and shot a dagger-sharp glance toward the street. Graben could see him listening carefully to the noise the riders made as they passed the hotel and to the creaking of saddle leather as they dismounted not far down the street.

A minute later a man slipped into the hotel, muttered something to the rancher and disappeared again.

Barlow spoke sharply to his daughter. "Stay here, Kate. Stay off the street and keep out of sight." He shifted his bright hard eyes back to Graben for a moment, seemed about to speak, then changed his mind and strode out of the hotel, his spurs making an angry fuss.

Graben heard the two women murmuring in low tones, but they seemed to have lost interest in him for the moment. He heard the name Rube Cushing mentioned, and then they fell silent, aware that Graben was watching them.

Kate Barlow's green eyes sparkled with dislike and anger and she started across the floor toward his table. "Kate," the Dauber woman said in a half warning, half pleading tone. But the younger woman ignored her and came on to Graben's table, sinking into the opposite chair with a kind of feline grace. He did not rise or remove his dusty black hat, but she did not seem surprised or offended by his lack of manners, as if she had expected no better from the likes of him. For a long moment she studied him in silence with her cool green eyes, and his narrow gray eyes, a good deal cooler, returned the appraisal while he continued his meal.

Then she asked in the blunt, rude tone he was coming to expect from everyone around here, "Who are you? What do you want here?"

"Not a thing," he said. "I was just passing through, and meant to keep going until everybody started telling me to keep moving. Now I may decide to stay a while."

"There's nothing here for you," she said. "It will just mean trouble if you stay here."

"Why?" he asked.

She seemed surprised by the question, and she gave him an almost startled look. The long dark lashes of her green eyes blinked at him, as if she were really seeing him for the first time. "Why?" she echoed.

Graben nodded, watching her curiously. "Why?" he repeated.

She thought about it for a moment, and then her lightly tanned face, with its natural rosy glow, got even redder, for it was obvious that she could not think of an adequate reply.

Seeing the predicament the girl was in, the Dauber woman came closer and said to Graben, "Star has been having a lot of trouble with rustlers lately. It's got so bad, whenever they see a strange rider, they think it might be another rustler. I imagine that's why you had that trouble with them today."

"You don't have to explain anything to him, Aunt Jill," Kate Barlow said resentfully.

Seeing the curious glance Graben divided between the two women, Jill Dauber smiled faintly and said, "Kate is my niece. Her mother was my sister."

"I knew she looked more like you than Whitey Barlow," he grunted. "Which is lucky for her."

Kate Barlow stiffened in her chair. "My father is a very handsome man," she informed him, "and I can remember when he was the most handsome man I ever saw. He's also the finest man I ever saw, whatever you may think of him."

"He could use a lesson in manners," Graben said. "Like you."

"Ha!" she said. "You're an odd one to talk about manners!"

Graben finished the roast beef, beans and potatoes and went to work on the apple pie. "I treat women like ladies who behave like ladies," he said, briefly raising his chilly gray eyes to glance at her.

"Ha!" she said again, but did not add anything this time.

Graben became aware that Jill Dauber was watching him with a faint smile. He got the feeling that she was beginning to like him. At least he hoped so, for he was beginning to like and admire her. The dry New Mexico climate had gone to work on her face, drying the skin and leaving a few wrinkles, but she was still a very attractive woman, and every inch a lady. By comparison, Kate Barlow behaved like a spoiled, rude child. And yet, in spite of himself, it was Kate Barlow who made Graben's heart beat a little faster. He had seen very few woman as physically attractive and exciting as she was, and he sensed a wild pulsing animal vitality in her that aroused his interest.

He finished the pie and sat back sipping his coffee, his chilly gray eyes watching her over the cup, his interest hidden behind the bleak reserve he showed the world, the watchful distrust he was not aware of showing.

"Can I get you some more coffee?" Jill Dauber asked.

"No thanks." He glanced at her and said quietly, "Somebody's a good cook."

Her eyes softened. She inclined her head slightly. "Thank you." It was not necessary for her to add who the cook was. Graben had seen no sign of any hired help and had already guessed that she did most of the work in the hotel, while Sam Dauber loafed at the desk—when he was not in the saloon down the street.

Graben set his empty cup down and reached for the birdshead Colt, intending to return it to his waistband.

Kate Barlow suddenly said, "Can I see that gun?" She sat tensely in her chair, watching him with wide green eyes, and Jill Dauber glanced uneasily at her and seemed to tense slightly also.

"Sorry," Graben said. The ghost of a smile twisted his thin lips. "You might become attached to it."

"That's not what you're afraid of," she said. "You're afraid I might use it on you."

Graben merely smiled again, that faint mocking smile so barren of warmth, faith or hope, and got to his feet, thrusting the birdshead Colt in his waistband. He glanced at Jill Dauber and started to reach in his pocket for money to pay for his supper.

"I can put it on your bill if you like," she said.

He slowly nodded and went by her.

"You better collect now," Kate Barlow said. "He may not be around long."

Graben glanced around, and realizing what she meant, he said, "You could be right."

As he left the hotel and headed for the Last Chance Saloon, he felt again the strange coldness in his gut that was like a warning of impending doom. He felt the cold lonely wind in his face, saw the horses tied before the saloon, and knew he would find no friends in the saloon. But he kept walking that way. He didn't think it mattered. If he didn't die tonight in Hackamore, he would die soon, somewhere.

Chapter 3

When he entered the saloon, Graben found two silent, separate groups of men, one at each end of the bar, with as much space as possible between the two groups. Whitey Barlow and his men were at the front end, eight of them in all, outnumbering the five men at the other end.

Just as Whitey Barlow dominated his group, the other group was dominated by a tall fat man with a smiling round face and bright yellow eyes. This fellow watched with interest as Graben walked around the Star men and stepped up to the bar in the open space between the two groups.

The bull-like Max Rumford glared at him with hatred in his bloodshot eyes, and Whitey Barlow said, "That ain't a very safe place."

Graben shrugged with apparent indifference and crooked his finger for a drink, with absolute confidence that he would get it, one way or another. "Nobody lives forever," he said, sounding bored.

Rube Cushing's round face lit up in a smile, and he said in a voice surprisingly soft and mild for so big a man, "You must be the feller everybody's talkin' about. I expected somebody with hair and horns. No offense, pilgrim, but you don't look very tough to me."

Graben gave him a cool gray glance and said quietly, "You better take a closer look."

Rube Cushing did take a closer look, and then he said in his soft, slow voice, "Yes, I think I see what you mean. I could use a man like you."

"Doing what?" Graben asked.

Rube Cushing chuckled and glanced at his men, who were grinning like a pack of wolves over a dead deer.

"Rustling my cows, that's what," Whitey Barlow said bluntly.

Rube Cushing grinned at Graben, and the grin was like a gloating admission, and an invitation to Graben to share the joke on a man Graben had every right to dislike.

"See, he don't even bother to deny it," the rancher said bitterly.

"Why should I deny it?" the fat man asked mildly. "You'd just call me a liar, and pretty soon one of us would have to be carried out of here."

"It wouldn't be me," Barlow said.

Ignoring the remark, Cushing again turned his relaxed, smiling attention to Graben, as if he had no other interest or care in the world. "What do you say, stranger? Me and the boys has got us a little camp in the hills west of here. Why don't you ride over and pay us a little visit before you leave. I think you'll find us a lot friendlier than some folks around here."

"That wouldn't surprise me," Graben said.

"Let me give you some good advice, Rube," Whitey Barlow said. "You and your boys keep away from this town and away from my cows."

The fat man merely smiled, showing no anger, and silently finished his drink. He nodded to his men and they quickly finished their own drinks. Cushing said to Graben, "Give it some thought," and then led his pack from the saloon, circling warily around the hard-eyed Star men.

Whitey Barlow cocked his head, listening to the creak of leather as Cushing and his men swung into their saddles and trotted their horses out of town. Then he turned his pale eyes and looked at Graben in the back-bar mirror. "Let me give you some good advice too," he said.

"Save it," Graben said, sipping at the glass of raw liquor Max Rumford had reluctantly set before him.

"Stay away from Rube Cushing and his men," Barlow said. "That bunch is all overdue for a rope."

"You're not trying to save my life, are you?" Graben asked in genuine surprise.

Whitey Barlow smiled a thin, twisted smile. "Not likely," he said. "I'm thinking of my men. Them rustlers ain't gonna let their necks be stretched without a fight. Old Rube's a lot tougher than he acts. They'll all fight like wolves when they're cornered. I just don't want you helping them, that's all."

"I see," Graben said, glancing down at his empty glass and idly wondering if another drink might thaw out the coldness in his belly.

"I also advise you to stay away from Sam Dauber till he sobers up," Barlow said. "I ain't worried about you, but I'd hate for Sam to get himself killed, if it worked out that way." There was an insincere smile on the rancher's lips as he said this, and unmistakable relish in his voice as he added, "He may be laying for you in a alley right now. The smart thing for you to do would be to ride out before he puts a bullet in you. Him or somebody else. You've already made so many enemies in this town, it don't look like I'll need to worry about you."

"You better keep worrying," Graben said. "I may decide to come after you for all the trouble you've caused me."

"You better let well enough alone and start riding before it's too late," Barlow warned him. "You've got everybody around here good and mad at you, and you're liable to find yourself dodging lead when you least expect it."

"If that happens, I'll know it was your fault for warning everyone against me," Graben said. "And it's liable to make me awful sore. I'm getting sore just thinking about it."

Whitey Barlow shrugged uncomfortably. At the moment he seemed less dangerous than any of the silent, hostile faces watching Graben in the back-bar mirror, and far less dangerous than the saloonkeeper, Max Rumford, who never took his bloodshot eyes off Graben.

"I only tried to put the run on you because I figgered you were a rustler," the rancher said. "Now I'm fairly sure you ain't—not yet anyway. Just see that you don't become one."

He finished his drink, wiped a rough hand across his mouth and spoke rather sharply to his men. "Let's go. Long day tomorrow."

In the back-bar mirror Graben saw those hard-bitten men exchange puzzled glances, for it was the slack season of the year when there was little work to be done on most ranches. But they silently followed Barlow out, mounted up and walked their horses along the street. They paused before the hotel and Graben heard the rancher call his daughter's name. Going to the batwing doors, he saw her leave the hotel, step astride her horse and ride out with the others.

Returning to the bar, Graben scowled at the huge saloonkeeper.

"What the hell you staring at?" he grunted.

Rumford shrugged his heavy shoulders. "You better keep away from her," he said. "If Whitey Barlow even catches you lookin' at his daughter, what's happened so far won't even be a sample."

"Real friendly little town you've got here," Graben said dryly.

For nearly half a minute Max Rumford stared at him in silence. Then the big man cleared his throat and rumbled, "One thing has always puzzled me about men like you. You're prob'ly purty fast with that gun you carry in your waistband. You may even be fast as greased lightning. But what makes you think somebody won't shoot you in the back?"

"Somebody probably will, sooner or later," Graben said, once more noticing the cold spot in his belly. It never really left him, but he had gotten so used to it that at times he did not notice it was there.

"It may be sooner than you think," Max Rumford told him, a look of undisguised hatred in the bloodshot eyes. "Nobody asked you to come here, and if you hang around here very long you're sure to end up dead. And nothing won't ever be done about it either. The nearest sheriff is over a hundred miles away, on the other side of them mountains, and he won't ever even hear about it. No one will tell him, and even if he did find out about it somehow and come around asking questions, he wouldn't find out anything. Around here we stick together and we don't like it when outsiders come in here and start causing trouble. Your're causing trouble just by being here, and sooner or later someone is just sure to put a stop to it."

"You, maybe?"

Again Rumford shrugged. "It could be me. It could be almost anybody. It might turn out to be the last person you'd ever expect."

Frank Graben's eyes, already cold, got even colder.

"Offhand, I can't think of very many people around here I'd trust behind my back. Judging by the ones I've seen so far."

"That's just what I mean," Rumford said. "Most of the folks around here are good people, except them rustlers. But you can push anybody too far."

"You better tell them that," Graben snapped, scowling angrily. "They're the ones who started pushing. I was just passing through, minding my own business, and everybody was all set to run me out of town before I even got here!"

Max Rumford remained unperturbed, his stubborn hatred undiminished. "Like I said before, nobody asked you to come here. We just want to be let alone here— ”

"That's all I want!"

"— and outsiders always bring trouble with them."

"You're all outsiders yourselves!" Graben said in angry amazement. "I rode through here seven or eight years back and there wasn't even a town here, or a ranch, or anything else. There wasn't a white man in this whole country. Now you people have moved in and claimed everything and you want to keep everyone else out. Well, I'll tell you what I told Whitey Barlow. You can all go to hell as far as I'm concerned!"

He slapped a coin on the bar and turned to leave, watching the saloonkeeper over his shoulder. Rumford looked, as usual, like a red-eyed bull getting set to charge. But he remained tensely poised that way behind his bar and silently watched Graben leave the saloon.

On his way back to the hotel, Graben kept to the darkest shadows at the edge of the street, not wanting to silhouette himself in the open. Only a few of the buildings along the deserted street showed lights. He got the uneasy feeling that silent, unseen men crouched behind the dark windows of the other buildings, watching every move he made, every step he took.

He remembered something Max Rumford had said. "It could be anybody. It might turn out to be the last person you'd ever expect." It might also be somebody he had never even seen, Graben thought bleakly, for that was the kind of town this was.

Then he thought about Sam Dauber who, according to what Whitey Barlow had said, might even now be laying for him in an alley. Dauber had not struck him as a very dangerous man, but you never could tell what a man might do when he got to drinking and brooding, and those quiet, meek little men sometimes turned out to be the worst killers once they got started.

Graben stopped with his back to a dark building and his sharp, narrow glance swept the empty street, probing the shadows between the buildings and passing on. His hand rested for a moment on the rosewood grip of the pistol in his waistband. The gun had a short barrel, four and a half inches, and limited stopping power. He liked it all right for close range, as inside a building, when he could shoot for the head or the heart. But now he longed for one of his more powerful and reliable Russians, considered by many to be the best pistols ever made.

Worse yet, he had no cartridges with him except for the five in the cylinder, there being an empty chamber under the hammer. What was he trying to do, he wondered, get himself killed?

The cold wind blew dust and tumbleweeds along the dark street, and some of the dust found its way into his bleak slitted eyes. The lonesome sound of the wind was in his ears, sometimes a soft sigh scarcely louder than a whisper, sometimes rising to a mournful wail. He thought about the farm in Missouri where he had grown up and where the sun had always been too hot or the wind too cold. He thought about his brother Tom, whom he had not seen in ten years and probably would never see again, and the loneliness in him grew. It would be nice if Tom were here now. Together they could take on the whole town.

Then he remembered that he had never been able to get along with Tom any better than he had with the rest of the world. Even if Tom were here, it was very possible that by now he would have made peace with these people, most of whom probably were, after all, not bad people in their way. It was even possible that he would be telling Frank to calm down and start thinking straight. Tom had told him that on more than one occasion when they were boys and Frank had lost his temper—never at any time a very hard thing for him to do. Tom had been the calm, steady one and had always seemed to have himself and the situation under control, whatever the situation happened to be. And it was a very rare occasion indeed when he had showed any sign of weakness or discouragement. Tom had always believed that everything would work out all right in the end, even though nothing much had ever worked out right in that unfortunate family or on that impoverished farm where Tom himself had once admitted with a bleak grin that they never failed to raise at least a hundred bushels of rocks to the acre. Yet he had never lost his faith in happy endings, not even after their parents died and they had to sell the worthless farm.

Well, I hope you found your happy ending, Tom, Frank thought, while he ran his eyes along the street, watching for some unseen enemy who might be planning a quick but not very happy ending for Frank himself.

But he could not remain here all night, watching and listening. He stepped away from the dark building and started along the edge of the street, avoiding the noisy boardwalk. When he had gone three steps, muzzle flame stabbed from a dark alley across the narrow street and the crash of a rifle shattered the silence. It seemed to Graben that he was already turning in that direction, whipping up the .41 Colt and firing back, when he heard the rifle slug hit the wall of the building behind him.

He fired twice, two shots that sounded almost like one, and then he heard feet pounding away down that narrow alley across the street. He ran across the dust with his gun raised for a third shot. He did not charge blindly into the alley. Even in moments of reckless anger he was too old and cautious a hand for that. Flattening himself against one of the buildings, he peered carefully around the corner, but saw nothing along the narrow alley that resembled a man. Listening, he heard no further sound. The man with the rifle had either stopped or was moving a lot more quietly.

Graben considered quickly. To go after a rifleman in the dark, in a strange town, was never a very smart thing to do. The man might be waiting for him almost anywhere. Graben preferred to try to find out who the man was and settle accounts with him later.

He felt all but certain that it was one of three men—Max Rumford, Barney Ludlow or Sam Dauber. Since he had just left Rumford in the saloon, that narrowed it down to Dauber and Ludlow, if his theory was right.

He pictured the two men in his mind. Barney Ludlow, short and potbellied, with his stubborn bulldog face. Graben almost grinned at the thought of Ludlow running through dark alleys with a rifle. It was an amusing picture, but he doubted if it was a very accurate one. Ludlow would be more likely to stand and fight, try to finish what he had started even if it got him killed.

Then Graben thought of Sam Dauber, a rather slight man, and no doubt still capable of a quick burst of speed if he needed to get away from someplace in a hurry. Graben remembered the wild look he had seen in the hotel man's eyes, the clammy sweat on his pale face. Dauber struck him as a man who might panic if his first shot missed—provided he ever worked up the courage to fire that first shot. Perhaps, Graben thought, turning his eyes toward the hotel, Dauber had found the courage in a bottle.

Graben headed for the hotel in long strides, ramming the pistol in his waistband as he stepped up on the veranda. He opened the door and pushed into the lobby, where he found Jill Dauber standing behind the desk. She was standing behind the empty chair where her husband usually sat. Her hands were white from gripping the back of the chair and her face seemed pale in the uncertain light from the lamp on the desk. She stood slim and straight and rigid, watching him with worried eyes.

"Where's Dauber?" he asked, the harsh sound of his voice making him aware of the cold rage seething inside him. He was about ready to declare war on the whole town, on the whole country, but he wanted to start with the man who had fired that shot at him from the alley. Not that he expected to find Dauber here. That was what he wanted to find out. If Dauber was hare, it would be proof that he could not have fired the shot.

Jill Dauber's eyes went to the closed door, near the bottom of the stair. "He's in there asleep," she said. After a moment she added, "Or passed out."

Graben stared at her with cold, suspicious eyes, seeing her for the first time as an enemy. Long ago he had lost patience with wives and mothers who lied to protect husbands and sons who deserved the worst that could happen to them. "Are you sure?" he asked.

She nodded, watching his face with frightened eyes. "Why do you ask?"

"Somebody took a shot at me a few minutes ago," he said, watching her closely. "And I'm pretty sure it was your husband."

She shook her head. "But that's impossible. I found him in there asleep thirty minutes ago, and he's been there ever since."

Graben's lips twisted in a cold, sarcastic smile. "I ain't been gone thirty minutes, and he wasn't here when I left."

She took a deep breath, her eyes widening a little. But then she met his glance and said calmly, "I think he was here then. He must have slipped in and went to his room when we were in the dining room. It's not unusual for him to do that when he's been drinking. Anyway, I found him in there asleep right after you left."

"In that case, it won't hurt if I take a look, will it?" Graben said dryly, and started around the desk.

She stepped quickly in front of the closed door, blocking his way and looking up at him with wide alarmed eyes. "Please don't go in there," she said, almost whispering. "If you go in there and he wakes up, there's going to be bad trouble."

"There's already bad trouble," Graben said in a harsh, angry voice. "Somebody just tried to kill me!"

"It wasn't my husband," she said. And then she added, with a noticeable reluctance, "He hasn't got the guts to kill anyone."

"Maybe not when he's sober. But I saw Whitey Barlow again at the saloon and he warned me that Dauber might be laying for me in an alley. Then right after I leave the saloon somebody takes a shot at me. What do you expect me to think?"

"I don't know why Whitey would say a thing like that," she said. "He should know Sam better than that."

"There's only one way you can prove to me that it wasn't him," Graben said flatly. "Open that door or call him out here."

"That's the last thing I want to do," she said, again lowering her voice. "I'm keeping my fingers crossed hoping he won't wake up and hear you saying such things about him. He probably wouldn't do anything when he's sober, but when he's been drinking there's no telling what he might do."

"He might even take a shot at me!" Graben said bitterly.

Jill Dauber bit her pale lips and seemed on the verge of bursting into tears. Seeing the strain and sheer torture in her face, he groaned under his breath and tramped up the stairs to his room.

Chapter 4

In his room, Graben made sure the curtain was closed, then lit the coal oil lamp and reloaded the birdshead Colt, tucking the little gun under the pillow. He removed his hat and boots, blew out the lamp, and stretched out on the bed, staring at the dark ceiling with bitter eyes.

He still was not certain whether it was Sam Dauber who had tried to kill him, but he was certain of one thing. Whoever it was, there would be someone who would swear he had been somewhere else at the time of the shooting. Graben had run into this sort of thing before and the pattern was familiar.

The anger still burned within him, generating enough heat to dispel temporarily the cold feeling that had been in his gut. But that was not much comfort. He did not need the cold feeling to know that he was lost. Whatever happened, whether he lived or died, there was no hope for him. He had always been at war with himself and the rest of the world and that was a war no man could win.

He was sinking into one of those bitter black moods where nothing mattered and he no longer cared much what happened. He had to watch himself when he got like that. Usually the best thing to do was to get off by himself as quickly as possible before he did something he would regret when the mood had passed. But that was exactly what he had been trying to do when he had run into Whitey Barlow and his men at the waterhole. It seemed that everywhere he went he ran into somebody who regarded his very existence as a personal insult.

There was no point in trying to ride away from trouble. Wherever he went he would find it waiting for him.

And right now he was in no mood to try to avoid it. He wanted to buckle on the Smith & Wessons and start shooting at the slightest provocation.

There was a little knock at the door, a slight sound but startling to a man who expected no callers unless it was someone who had come to kill him.

Graben's hand went under the pillow for the birdshead Colt and he rose from the bed in one smooth, soundless movement. In his socks he crossed the floor, blew the light out and then faced the door with the gun held ready. "Yes?" he said, and stepped quickly aside, half expecting the caller to start shooting through the door at the sound of his voice.

"It's me," Jill Dauber said. "Can I talk to you for a minute?"

Graben shot the bolt, opened the door to make sure she was alone, then turned his back on her and grunted, "I'll light the lamp." He found a match, lit the lamp and then turned to find her standing at the door, watching him.

"Do you think you'll need that?" she asked, glancing at the gun in his hand.

He scowled and rammed the gun into his waistband. "I'd offer you a chair," he said dryly, "but there don't seem to be one."

"Oh, I forgot," she said, coming farther into the room but leaving the door open. "I was going to get a chair out of the one of the other rooms for you. I can do that now if you like."

"It's not important," he said. "Unless you want one to sit in."

"I'm only going to stay a minute," she said, and then was silent for almost that long. "I don't really know how to begin."

"If it's about your husband," he grunted, sitting down on the bed, "I think we might as well drop it."

She looked at him with still eyes. "You don't believe what I said down there, do you?"

He shrugged. "What difference does it make? I'm not going to bother him until I find out for sure it was him took that shot at me. And I don't guess there's much danger of me finding that out now, is there?"

She made a slow circle about the room, studying the worn carpet. "I don't know any way I can convince you I was telling the truth," she said. "If I'd known for sure he was still asleep, I would have let you take a look. But I was afraid he was awake and waiting in there with a gun. Scared and half drunk—I was afraid if you went in that room he might shoot you just out of fear."

Graben sighed wearily and ran his fingers back through his hair. He suddenly felt tired and wished she would go so he could try to get some sleep.

Watching him, she said, "You still don't believe me, do you?"

"I don't know what to believe," he said. "All I know is, the next time somebody takes a shot at me, they better make the first one count."

"That's what I wanted to talk to you about," she said. "I've got a feeling that whoever took that shot at you wasn't trying to hit you. It was probably just a warning for you to leave town. But the next time they may try to hit you."

Graben glanced up at her, his lips twisting in a bitter smile. "And you're going to try to get me to leave before that happens."

After a moment she nodded, looking a little embarrassed. "That was the idea. If you stay here there's bound to be trouble. And one way or another Sam is bound to get involved in it, since you're staying here at the hotel. The others will keep after him until he has to take a stand."

"I have a very strong feeling that he's already involved," Graben said. "Even if he didn't take that shot at me, he's been talking war."

"That was the whiskey talking," Jill Dauber said, her eyes worried.

The humorless smile returned briefly to Graben's bleak weathered face. "Maybe it was the whiskey that took that shot at me."

She sighed, but said nothing for a long moment. She seemed lost in thought. "Sam isn't much, but he's all I've got." She was apparently going to say more, but Graben bluntly interrupted.

"He's not good enough for you. Or man enough."

Jill Dauber looked at him in surprise. Then she smiled a small, tired smile. "What do you know about it?" she asked.

"I've got eyes," he said.

She continued to smile the small, tired smile and was silent, looking at herself in the bureau mirror.

"How old are you?" Graben asked suddenly.

She looked startled, then shook her head. "Too old."

"Forty?"

"Do I look that old?" she asked, a look of surprise and disappointment in her eyes. She studied her face in the mirror, and said sadly,

"I suppose I do. This country's hard on women."

"How old are you?"

"Thirty-seven. Not that it makes much difference. I'll be forty soon enough." Then she looked at him curiously. "How about you? How old are you?"

"Twenty-seven."

Again she looked surprised, even a little disappointed. "Is that all? You look older. I've been a little unhappy thinking you were probably a few years younger than me, and you're ten whole years younger. Not that it matters, of course."

"Of course not."

She looked at him uncertainly. "I don't know how that sounded. What I meant was, I'm a happily married woman, and you wouldn't be interested even if I weren't."

"I wouldn't say that."

She stood looking at herself in the mirror as if she had not heard him. "Especially after you've seen Kate. I think she's even more beautiful than her mother was."

"Her mother dead?"

Jill nodded. "She died a long time ago, when she wasn't much older than Kate is now. She was five years older than me, but she always seemed so healthy and full of life. I just know she'd outlive me, but you never really know who'll be the first to go."

Graben was silent, looking at the floor. The icy claw had closed around his guts again, like the cold hand of death.

"I better get back downstairs," Jill Dauber said, "before Sam wakes up. I don't want to cause the very trouble I'm trying to avoid."

Graben rubbed his hands together, a tight grin on his face. "I keep wondering what would happen if I kissed you," he said. "Since you're trying so hard to avoid trouble, I could take advantage of you awful easy."

"You could," she said, "but you won't."

He looked up at her in wonder. "What makes you think that?"

She met his glance directly. "I can tell. You've killed and you'll probably kill again, but you wouldn't bother a decent woman."

"Not unless I thought she wanted to be bothered," he said.

Jill Dauber's eyes were thoughtful, her face strangely blank. She was silent for a moment, and then she said, "I think I better go."

"Good night."

She left the room without answering.

Well, Graben thought, you just made a damn fool out of yourself.

After he blew the light out and went to bed, it was not Jill Dauber that he thought about, but Kate Barlow.

At breakfast the next morning Graben had the dining room to himself. There was no one at the desk when he came downstairs; he saw no signs of Sam Dauber. And he had been sitting in the silent empty dining room for several minutes before Jill Dauber appeared from the kitchen. He thought she had washed her hair or spent a lot of time brushing it, and she was wearing a different dress that accented the curves of her slender body. Her face looked younger somehow, the skin did not seem as dry and tight, the faint signs of premature aging were less noticeable. There were spots of color in her cheeks. She seemed flushed and pale at the same time—and beautiful. But there was a look of dread in her eyes and she seemed to have trouble meeting his glance.

"What would you like?" she asked, and he did not miss the fact that she offered no greeting of any kind. She did not seem overjoyed to see him.

He deliberately assumed an air of casual indifference, barely glancing at her, and she seemed to relax a little. "Whatever you've got," he said. "Plenty of black coffee's the main thing."

"It'll be a few minutes," she said and went back into the kitchen.

Graben glanced out the window and regarded the street with bleak gray eyes. The weathered, unpainted buildings across the street showed the reddish glow of the rising sun and there should have been some activity along the street, but there was none. He saw no one. The town was silent and seemed to be waiting for something—waiting perhaps for him to leave so it could resume its humdrum existence.

Jill Dauber brought his breakfast and was on the point of retreating when he said, "Where's the crowd?"

She glanced through the window at the empty street and shook her head, a dull look in her eyes. "There probably won't be anyone."

Graben looked at her with his bleak eyes. "Because of me?"

The spots of color reappeared in her cheeks that made her seem younger and almost beautiful. But her face showed a little strain and discomfort. After a moment she slowly nodded.

"And that's mainly how you make your living, isn't it?" he asked. "By feeding people?"

Again she nodded. "A big part of the time all those rooms upstairs are empty. There's no one up there now but you."

Graben's eyes narrowed slightly. "Your husband told me yesterday that he didn't have any rooms for rent."

She flushed. "That's what Whitey Barlow sent word for him to say."

"Whitey Barlow own everyone in this town?" Graben asked.

A look of distress had come into Jill Dauber's flushed face. She suddenly looked years older. "He doesn't own anyone," she said. "But if it wasn't for Star, this town would dry up and die, and everyone knows that. So Whitey pretty much has everything his way around here."

Graben went to work on his bacon and eggs, his dark brows slightly raised over narrow pale eyes. "It looks to me like Barlow's doing the town a lot more harm than good," he said. "There's room enough in this country for half a dozen ranches. How long does he think he can keep everyone else out?"

Jill Dauber looked out at the empty street and folded her arms. "It probably does seem like he's hurting the town by trying to keep others out," she said. "But it's not as simple as it seems. A few small outfits have already tried to move in, but they couldn't make a go of it or pay their bills. They either left or started living on Star beef and Whitey ran them out. Now a new family has moved into one of the old deserted shacks over west of here, some people named Wilkins, a couple with a nearly grown daughter. Whitey has let them alone so far because of the girl and her mother, but how they intend to make a living is anybody's guess. They haven't got any stock, just two work horses, and that place is too rocky to farm. And then there's Rube Cushing and his bunch up in the hills west of them—everyone knows Rube and his men are rustlers, living on Star beef. There's been so much trouble with them and nearly everyone else who's come into this country, the townspeople have decided we were better off when there wasn't anyone here but Star."

"That why everybody was so happy to see me?" Graben asked.

She slowly nodded. "That's part of it. But you must have done something to make Whitey awful sore. That's the first time he's ever asked the whole town not to do any business with a stranger passing through."

"I think his problem was that I didn't get down on my knees," Graben said. "I didn't kneel before the king."

"That could be it," she admitted. "Whitey sees himself as an important man and he resents any show of disrespect. And if you made him look bad in front of his hands, he'll never forgive you."

"I hope not," Graben said. Then he asked, "Where's Dauber?"

"He hasn't got up yet," she said in a different tone. "He hardly ever gets up before eight or nine o'clock, even when he's not drinking. He usually stays up late and then sleeps late. He sleeps in the small room behind the lobby where he can hear anyone come in. I sleep in the room by the kitchen so I won't disturb him when I get up."

Graben ate in silence, his attention apparently on his food. For a moment he almost wondered if she was trying to tell him more than she was actually saying, but he dismissed the notion as absurd. She was a lady, and not likely to take an interest in a cold-eyed gunfighter. Yet he could not help wondering. Sam Dauber was obviously not much of a husband or much of a man, and she probably got lonely at times, lady or not.

Jill Dauber coughed. "Can I get you some more coffee or anything?"

He glanced at his half-empty cup. "You could warm it up."

She went into the kitchen and returned with the coffeepot. He watched her refill his cup with the smoking black liquid, and then he looked up at her and asked, "You still want me to leave?"

She flushed. Her eyes were strangely soft, but she met his glance for only a moment before looking away. "I think it would be best," she said. "For your sake as well as everyone else's."

Graben sighed. He lifted the cup and sipped his coffee in silence, watching the street through the window.

Jill Dauber studied his face for a moment, and then she took the coffeepot back to the kitchen. Graben set his cup down and lit a cigar. When the woman returned a few minutes later with a cup of coffee for herself and sat down at the next table, he glanced at her and asked, "You mind if I smoke?"

"Go ahead." She gave him a fleeting smile. "Everyone else does."

Then for a few minutes they both sat watching the street in silence through the window. Graben knew he should be going, yet he hated to leave. It was partly because he did not want the people around here to think they had scared him away, but that was not the only reason.

He glanced at Jill Dauber, scowling a little, resenting her for arousing his interest against his will. Nothing could come of it, or if anything did come of it, it would cause him more trouble than it was worth.

She returned his glance and seemed puzzled by the expression on his face, the coldness of his gray eyes. After a moment she asked, "Have you decided yet?"

"Decided what?"

"When you're going to leave."

A bitter smile crossed his face. "You're just like everyone else in this town. You can't wait to get rid of me."

"It's not that," she said. "If things were different, I'd be glad for you to stay as long as you want to."

Graben looked at her and she did not look away. Not even when the spots of red appeared in her cheeks. Graben was the first to look away. He looked out at the street. If things were different. How often had he wished things were different?

He had hoped things would be different here. Things were different all right, but not the way he had hoped.

Jill Dauber cleared her throat, a sound he did not particularly care for. But when she looked at him her green-hazel eyes were gentle and a little sad. "Is it this way everywhere you go?" she asked.

He scowled at her. "What gave you that idea?"

She swallowed. "Just a feeling."

After a moment he said in a harsh bitter voice, "It's about the same. Maybe not quite this bad some places."

For what seemed a long time Jill Dauber sat sipping her coffee in silence and watching the street through the window. Then she said, "I've changed my mind. As far as I'm concerned you can stay here as long as you please. You have as much right to be here as anyone else."

Graben watched her for a long moment and neither of them moved or even seemed to breathe. Then he let out a long breath through his teeth and got to his feet. "How much do I owe you?" he said.

She blinked in surprise. "You're leaving?"

He sighed. "I think I'd better."

She sat watching him with a strange half-puzzled look in her eyes, and then she said softly, "Don't go because of me."

He regarded her thoughtfully. "You know there will be trouble if I stay here."

"I know," she said. "But somehow I don't much care anymore. I've just been thinking about my life here. It's nothing. Whatever happens—well, at least it will be something."

Frank Graben stood there watching her for a long time. He did not say anything.

CHAPTER 5

There was a small barbershop in town. Graben entered the dim room and found a small pink-cheeked man sitting in the chair reading an old magazine. The little man peered at him with dread and then scampered out of the chair. Graben sat down and said, "Shave and a haircut. But I don't want it to look like my hair was cut, see?"

The little barber gaped at him in amazement. "Oh, all right! I'll try!"

While nipping cautiously at the hair around Graben's ears, the barber wondered aloud why he didn't want folks to know he'd let his hair be cut. "Not that it's any of my business," he hastened to add.

"It's not any of theirs either," Graben told him.

"I see," the pink-cheeked barber said. But the puzzlement did not leave his face. Clearly he suspected some deep mystery here. What was Graben trying to hide? Why would anyone wish to conceal the fact that he had got his hair cut? It was not as if it was a shameful thing to do, nor a violation of any law that he had every heard of. Nearly everyone got their hair cut at one time or another, though the Lord knew there were men who put it off as long as they could, as if they were trying to put a poor barber out of business.

"I know! You've got friends who don't like barbers and you don't want them to know you let one cut your hair. Is that it?"

"No," Graben said, boredly watching the street.

"I see."

The barber worked in silence for a time.

"You make a bet with someone that you wouldn't get your hair cut?"

"No."

"I see."

Graben shifted in the chair, and the little barber jerked the scissors away lest he make a slip and cut off so much hair it would be noticeable.

"Ain't you afraid Whitey Barlow won't like it if he finds out you cut my hair?" Graben asked with a sour grin.

"So that's it!" the little barber exclaimed. "You were thinking of me all the time! You were afraid Whitey would get sore at me if he could tell you'd got your hair cut! That's mighty considerate of you, mister! Yes sir!"

Graben scowled but said nothing. There was no point in talking to a fool.

When the barber had finished, Graben critically examined the results in the mirror, and then scowled murderously at the beaming little man. "I can't even tell I've had a haircut," he said.

The barber's face fell. "But didn't you say—"

"Never mind. How much do I owe you?"

"About four bits, I guess. That's my usual fee for a haircut and a shave. But just make it two bits this time, seeing as how the haircut wasn't up to your liking."

Graben bleakly studied his leathery face in the mirror. "Shave wasn't much either."

The barber scratched his chin. "Er—well, I won't charge you anything this time."

Graben turned and looked at him through cold slitted eyes. The little barber backed off a step. Graben said, "A man in your line of work must hear all the local gossip."

The barber backed away another step. "Well, I wouldn't say that."

"It wouldn't surprise me," Graben went on, "if you don't already know who took that shot at me last night. Especially since it came from the alley just outside your bedroom window."

The barber's eyes widened in alarm. "It was dark! I couldn't see anything! And I was afraid to look! Afraid whoever it was would kill me!"

"You were afraid, all right. But you looked. Maybe not when you heard the shot, but before, when you heard him go by your window."

The little barber hung his head humbly, submissively. "It's true. I did sneak over to the window to peek out. But I didn't see anyone. I would of had to open the window and stick my head out, and I was too scared. I knew there was somebody out there and I was afraid they meant to break in and rob me. Maybe even kill me! I'm all alone here at night and you can't imagine how scared I was. I crawled under the bed and stayed there. Then when I heard the shot—you can't imagine how loud it sounded. My ears are still ringing. I thought I was going to have a heart attack. Then somebody else come charging across the street firing back at him and one of the bullets came through the wall and only missed me by about a foot. I thought I was going to be killed for sure." He ran an unsteady hand back over his thinning colorless hair and shook his head. "I sure hope I don't have to go through another night like last night again anytime soon."

"You ain't heard any talk?"

"How could I? You're the first person I've seen since then."

Graben handed him a coin. "Keep your eyes and ears open—and your mouth shut. From now on you'll do all your talking to me, you understand?"

"S-sure. Whatever you say."

Graben put on his black hat and left the barbershop, and the barber looked at the coin in his hand. It was a twenty-dollar gold piece.

Graben walked down the street to the livery stable. Barney Ludlow came out and stared at him through mean hard eyes. There was a stubborn set to the chunky man's bulldog face. He remained sulkily silent. Graben glanced at the fellow's potbelly and felt a perverse desire to kick it. But he controlled the impulse. He had more important things on his mind.

"I don't guess you happened to hear some shooting last night," he said in a casual, conversational tone.

Ludlow shook his head with grim relish. "Didn't hear a thing," he said. "I sleep mighty sound. Clear conscience, I guess."

"It probably comes from being so helpful and considerate to strangers," Graben told him.

Ludlow shrugged. "If you come for your horse, I'll get him for you. If not, I'll get back to my shovel."

"Don't let me keep you," Graben said. "I respect a man who knows his place."

Ludlow gave him a mean look, then turned and went back into the stable.

Graben had come mainly to check on his horse, and now went around to the corral in back and leaned against the pole fence, rolling and lighting a cigarette. Besides his blue roan there were half a dozen horses picking about the corral, hunting any bit of loose hay or grass. Most of the horses seemed half asleep, but as usual the blue roan's head was in the air and his dark eyes were bright and alive. He spotted Graben at once and stood watching him expectantly, but did not come toward him.

Ludlow emerged from the rear of the barn with a shovel in his hands and said flatly, "I don't want you hangin' around here, Graben. Move along."

Graben removed the cigarette from his mouth with his left hand and said, "I see you've been talking to Dauber."

"What's that supposed to mean?"

"I haven't told anyone my name. So he must have told you."

"So?"

"What else did he tell you?"

"I don't see where that's any of your business," Ludlow said.

"Somebody tried to kill me last night. That is my business."

Barney Ludlow smiled grimly. "If you've come here tryin' to find out who done it, you've come to the wrong place. I wouldn't tell you even if I knew."

"I figger it was either you or Sam Dauber," Graben said. "It could have been either one of you. If I can't find out which one of you it was, I may just decide to flip a coin and see which one of you loses."

Ludlow's eyes grew uneasy. "What's that supposed to mean?"

"You figger it out," Graben said, and turning his back on the man he returned to the street and strolled along it to the Last Chance Saloon. He flipped his cigarette into the dust before pushing in through the swing doors.

Max Rumford stood behind the bar with his big rump against the edge of the back bar. He glared at Graben through his bloodshot eyes and cleared his throat. It sounded like the low angry growl of some huge dog, and Graben decided that the bushy overhanging brows made Rumford resemble a dog almost as much as a bull, or perhaps a cross between the two. Then without a word the big man set out a bottle and a glass, and this time Graben poured his own drink.

After taking a sip of the raw liquor, Graben lowered the glass and said in a dry idle way, "Don't guess you heard any shooting last night."

Rumford shrugged his meaty shoulders. "I warned you something like that would happen," he said. "I was only surprised it happened so soon after I told you."

Graben took another sip of the raw liquor. "I don't guess you'd know who did it."

"It could of been anybody. Like I said last night."

"Anybody could wind up dead if it happens again," Graben told him.

Max Rumford propped his elbows on the bar and glared back at him with no sign of fear. "So could you," he said, as if savoring the thought.

Graben nodded. "It's possible," he admitted.

The saloonkeeper regarded him in silence for a time, then asked, "How are you and Jill Dauber getting along?"

Graben looked at him with cold gray eyes. "What's that supposed to mean?"

Rumford glanced toward the batwing doors and then said, "In case you make any time with her, don't let it go to your head. You wouldn't be the first. Jill Dauber has always been kind to strangers. I guess she always picks strangers because she thinks they won't tell anyone. But sometimes they come in here and joke about it. I've never told anyone till now, and I'm only telling you because I wouldn't want you to get the idea you're anything special."

Graben looked at his scowling dark face in the back-bar mirror. He tried to get angry with the saloonkeeper, but couldn't. He was more angry with himself than anyone else, for being such a simpleton. He had had some foolish notion that he was the first, that there had not been anyone before him.

He scowled at Rumford and asked, "You think Dauber knows about it?"

Rumford shrugged. "If he does he ain't never said anything to me about it, and I ain't said nothing to him. But he's a mighty unhappy man for some reason, and nearly anybody else around here would be mighty glad to trade places with him. Course, they prob'ly don't know her like he does."

Graben considered that in frowning silence.

"There's something else you might like to know," Rumford said with malicious satisfaction. "She lies about her age. She tells everyone she's thirty-seven, but Sam told me a while back she's thirty-nine."

"Maybe it was Sam who lied," Graben said.

"Why would he lie about a thing like that?" Rumford asked.

Graben shrugged. "Why would he tell you at all?"

Max Rumford considered that question for a time, but apparently he could not find an answer that pleased him.

"You got any cigars?" Graben asked.

Rumford shook his head. "Try the general store. They might even have some at the hotel, but it doubt it."

Graben laid a coin on the bar and turned to go. Then he thought of something and turned back. "One more thing. Do you think Whitey Barlow could have sent one of his men back last night to take that shot at me?"

Rumford shrugged. "Your guess is as good as mine. But if you want my opinion, it was somebody here in town. But maybe not who you think. It might of just been somebody trying to do Whitey a favor. He's got a lot of friends here."

"He can't have very many," Graben said. "He's already run nearly everybody out of the country, before they ever had a chance to become his friends."

"Whitey is particular about choosin' his friends," Rumford said.

"He don't seem too particular about choosing his enemies," Graben said. "I gather almost anyone will do that he doesn't know well."

Rumford did not say anything until Graben started to leave, and then he said, "Let me give you some advice. If you keep going around asking questions, somebody's liable to tell you something you don't want to hear."

"Like what?"

Rumford planted his elbows on the bar and glared at him from under the bushy gray brows. "Like to mind your own business."

Graben smiled faintly and left the saloon.

Sam Dauber stepped to the back door of the hotel and found Jill hanging Graben's black double-breasted shirt and black trousers on the clothesline. He began to tremble with anger. "What are you doing?" he cried hoarsely. "I won't have you washing his clothes, you hear!"

She looked around at him with cool hard eyes—an expression she never let anyone see but him. "I'd rather wash them than smell them," she said.

He saw that she had put on the dress that set off her figure to the best advantage, and spent maybe half the night on her hair and face, trying to make herself appear younger and more attractive. To him it was an old and bitter story. Let a handsome stranger check into the hotel and she immediately started trying to look her best, when she never bothered to for her husband!

"You stay away from him, you hear!" Dauber cried, trying to control his trembling voice. "And stay out of his room! I don't want you going upstairs for any reason while he's here!"

She gave him a contemptuous little smile and did not bother to reply.

Graben entered the general store and found a short, slight man with a large head behind the counter—a man in his fifties with thin graying hair, a strong stubborn jaw and hard dark eyes that glinted through rimless spectacles at Graben. According to the sign out front this was Goodman.

"You got any cigars?"

The storekeeper's teeth clicked together. His face was like wood. "Sorry. Fresh out."

Graben looked about and saw several boxes of cigars on the shelf. He walked over, selected a box, opened it and got a handful of cigars, then put the box back on the shelf and headed for the door, humming to himself.

Goodman's round alarmed dark eyes peered through his spectacles in amazement. "Hey, where are you going with those cigars?"

Graben glanced around at him and asked innocently, "What cigars? Didn't you just say you were fresh out?"

The storekeeper's mouth closed like a trap and Graben went on out. Goodman's eyes gleamed with hatred as he watched the tall man leave.

Graben paused on the boardwalk with his back to the store and lit one of the cigars. Goodman had not had his brand and he would not have taken them except to annoy the man. He glanced both ways along the street, which ran north and south. At the north edge of town the street separated into three trails leading across the desert, one going east, one north, one west. There was also a trail leading south from town but it did not appear to be used much. The one going north, evidently leading to Star headquarters, showed the most sign of travel.

There was even now a rider coming along the road from the north.

It turned out to be Kate Barlow, riding a beautiful reddish-yellow horse with a darker red mane and tail. She drew rein in the street before Graben, looked at him with her cool green eyes and said, "Well, I see you're still alive."

"So far."

"Don't let it go to your head," she told him. "If you stay here for very long it will be in Boot Hill."

"Where's that?" Graben asked with a show of interest.

She nodded her head south. "Just outside of town." Then she turned her green eyes curiously back to him, studied him thoughtfully. "Are you as big a fool as you seem?"

"I didn't know it showed."

"It shows all right," she said. "If you were smart you'd leave. You would have left already."

Graben took the cigar from his mouth, looked at it in mild disgust, then dropped it to the dust. "What's everyone around here so afraid of?" he asked.

"Not of you," she said. "I can tell you that much."

Graben looked at her with interest. "Is that why they hide in alleys and take shots at me with a rifle?" he asked. "Because they're not afraid of me?"

Her long dark lashes blinked once and then she studied him carefully. "When did that happen?"

"Last night right after you and the others left. I figgered you heard the shot."

She shook her head. "We were riding pretty fast. It's close to ten miles to the ranch."

Watching her closely, Graben added, "I even thought Whitey might have sent someone back to take that shot at me."

Her lightly tanned face flushed with anger and her thin lips tightened with resentment. She seemed on the point of saying something, but then Goodman came to the door of his store behind Graben and spoke to her.

"I didn't sell him those cigars, Kate. He just helped himself to a handful and then left without paying for them."

Kate Barlow looked at Graben with scornful eyes. "A common thief!"

"He said he didn't have any," Graben said. "I didn't figger a man should complain about a few cigars he didn't have in the first place."

She looked past him as if he were not there and said to the storekeeper, "Don't worry, Hiram," she said. "I'll see that you don't lose anything on the cigars."

"Thank you, Kate," the storekeeper said. "But I'm not worried about the cigars. I just didn't want Whitey to think I sold them to him."

"No, I think you should put them on Whitey's bill," Graben said. "If he's going to pick your customers for you, he should pay you for any losses."

"That's between Hiram and my father," Kate Barlow said resentfully. "It's no concern of yours."

"The hell it ain't," Graben said. "When your old man tells everyone not to sell me anything, then it's my concern."

"Why don't you just leave," she told him. "Nobody's asked you to stay here. Nobody asked you to come here."

"Did anybody ask Whitey to come here?"

"Nobody had to ask him," she said disdainfully.

"Nobody had to ask me either," Graben said. "I go wherever I please."

Her lips paled and she said in a quiet bitter voice as she reined her horse away, "You can go to hell for all I care."

"I intend to," Graben said. "But I'll have plenty of company."

She did not reply or look back, but reined her claybank over to the hotel rack and swung gracefully to the ground. Graben watched her tie the horse and enter the hotel. Then he glanced over his shoulder and found Hiram Goodman watching the hotel with hungry eyes. Graben bared his teeth in a wolfish grin. Goodman looked at him in alarm, then fled back inside and shut the door.

Graben crossed to the hotel. On the veranda he hesitated, then sat down in one of the chairs against the wall. He lit another cigar and smoked it with pretended relish, for he knew Hiram Goodman would be watching him through the window of his store.

A short time later Kate Barlow came out of the hotel, stepped off the veranda and untied her horse, trying not to notice Graben sitting in the chair. But she could not help saying, "Don't you know when you're not wanted?"

He rolled the cigar between his teeth. "I'm getting used to it. Makes me feel right at home."

She swung into the saddle and her cool green eyes went to Graben to see if he was watching her. He wasn't. He did not seem to be looking at anything in particular, unless it was something inside his head. His thoughts seemed far away.

"What do you want here?" she asked, with a bitterness in her tone that puzzled him.

"I came here looking for peace and quiet," he said.

"Ha!" she said.

"Since I didn't find it," he said in the same distant tone as before, "since I can't seem to find it anywhere, I'm seriously thinking about declaring war on everyone who causes me any trouble."

"How long do you think you'll last?" she asked.

"I don't know," he said. "I might last longer that way than if I just wait around for somebody to take another shot at me from an alley."

"It's too bad he wasn't a better shot," she said. "Whoever it was."

Graben regarded her curiously. "Why are you so bitter?"

"Everything was all right until you came here," she said. "We've had some trouble with squatters and rustlers, but nothing we couldn't handle. Then you show up with that cold look of death in your eyes."

Graben smoked in silence for a moment. "It worry you?"

"Yes, it worries me! I just know something bad will happen if you stay here. Why don't you go, before it's too late!"

Without waiting for a reply she turned the claybank and cantered out of town in a cloud of dust.

"It's already too late," Graben murmured to himself, when she was almost out of sight.

CHAPTER 6

Sam Dauber came out on the veranda and looked down toward the saloon with thirsty eyes, rubbing a hand across his mouth. Then he saw Graben sitting there in his black hat, brown corduroy coat and dark gray trousers. He did not see the gun in Graben's waistband but knew it was there, and he stared at the gunfighter with bitter bloodshot eyes. His face turned a sickly color and his shakes became more noticeable. He seemed on the point of saying something, but his courage failed him and he stepped carefully off the veranda and went unsteadily along the boardwalk to the saloon.

Looking after him with narrow gray eyes, Graben suddenly thought in surprise, He never took that shot at me last night. He was too drunk.

But if it had not been Dauber, who could it have been? Ludlow? If it was not one of those two, Graben had no idea who it could have been. Perhaps, as Max Rumford had warned him beforehand, it might be almost anyone in this town. It might even be Hiram Goodman, though Graben doubted it. Goodman did not strike him as the type.

It occurred to him that he was making a very good target where he sat right now for anyone in one of the buildings across the street, and there was no guarantee that the marksman would wait until dark to try again.

Graben tossed the half-smoked cigar into the street, rose and went into the hotel. The lobby was empty and he saw no sign of Jill

Dauber in the dining room when he passed the open door. He climbed the stairs to his room, hung his hat on a nail in the wall and stepped over to the window, parting the curtain and looking down at the lifeless street. Then for a time he studied the false fronts of the buildings across the street.

He had left the door unlocked and presently he heard it open. He wheeled with a gun in his hand and saw Jill Dauber standing there. He scowled and put the gun away, saying, "That's a good way to get shot."

She closed the door and stood with her back to it, watching his face carefully. "I was just going to straighten up a little," she said. "I didn't know you'd come back in or I would have knocked." He did not reply and she added, "I washed your black shirt and pants. They should be dry by around noon."

"You shouldn't have bothered."

"I probably shouldn't have," she agreed in a different tone. "Sam didn't like it. You better watch out for him. I think he's working himself up to do something foolish."

Graben thought about what Max Rumford had said, and he turned back to the window. "I guess he's getting tired of it," he said, with his back to her, looking down at the street.

"What do you mean?" she asked.

He shrugged. "Nothing." He moved away from the window, started to sit down on the bed, then changed his mind and remained standing, not looking at her.

"Is something wrong?" she asked, watching his face.

"Not much. Just everything." He reached for his hat. "If you're going to straighten up in here I better get out of your way."

"Oh, there's no hurry about that," she said quickly. "I can do that later." After a moment she added, "Sam went to the saloon. No telling when he'll come back."

Was she trying to tell him something? Graben was silent, looking down at the hat in his hand, his dark brows somber over hooded gray eyes.

She cleared her throat and said, "When he comes back I guess he'll be stinking drunk again. Sometimes he won't touch a drop for weeks at a time, but once he gets started it's hard to get him to stop. And when he's drinking, he's hard to live with."

Graben glanced at her. He noticed that she seemed rather plain— and old—after seeing Kate Barlow so radiant and beautiful in the sunlight, her smooth tan cheeks rosy with a healthy glow. Also with anger, he sadly admitted.

Jill Dauber smiled as if inviting Graben to share a private joke. "Sometimes I don't know what I'm going to do with that man anyway."

Graben overlooked the familiarity, but kept his own distance. "Didn't you know what he was like when you married him?"

She shook her head, her smile fading. "I had no idea what he was like when I married him. I thought I did. He seemed like the nicest man I'd ever met. That was what he wanted me to think. It was quite a while before I found out what he was really like. It doesn't show till he starts drinking."

Graben offered no comment, and Jill Dauber studied him with anxious eyes. She seemed puzzled by the change in him. He no longer seemed interested in her. He could have told her it was because he could not get the picture of Kate Barlow out of his mind, and because of what Max Rumford had said. He could have, but he didn't and he knew he never would.

As she watched him, some small hope seemed to fade from Jill Dauber's eyes. She looked older, plainer, the lines in her face more noticeable. There was a quiet weariness in her tone as she said, "Well, I better get back downstairs. I've got a lot of work to do. And Sam may come back sooner than I expect."

After she had left, Graben found himself doubting if she had actually come up here to straighten up his room. There had been some other reason. But Graben did not much care what it was. He was no longer interested in Jill Dauber.

He had made the same mistake here that he had made in other places. He had suddenly become interested in one particular woman and lost interest in all others. And here, as elsewhere, it had turned out to be the one woman he could not have. Kate Barlow.

He glanced at his face in the bureau mirror—an unusually handsome face in a rugged, completely masculine way. But that was not what people noticed. It was the grim weathered hardness of the face that they noticed, and the hawklike fierceness of the bleak cold gray eyes over the bony, slightly aquiline nose. There was no peace in that face, no humor or warmth or trust. Just that predatory, hawklike watchfulness.

He remembered what Kate Barlow had said, "...that cold look of death in your eyes." That was what she had seen. Not the wave in his copper-tinged dark hair, or the lean rugged grandeur of the face in profile. It was the frowning brow, the cold slitted gray eyes that she had noticed. She did not know it was men like her father and the people of this town that had made him that way, and she would not have listened if he had told her.

He stretched out on the bed with a weary sigh, thinking again that the smart thing for him to do would be to ride on. He had no friends here, only enemies. A word from Whitey Barlow had turned the whole town against him even before he arrived, and his own attitude had not helped. The situation was not likely to improve either. It would only get worse. The hostility and resentment among the townspeople and the Star riders would grow, and if he hung around he stood a good chance of stopping a bullet.

But he was tired of riding and his horse was tired. Both badly needed a few days' rest before setting out on the trail again. And he no longer had much hope that it would be any better in the next town, wherever that was. He had been in too many towns and nowhere had he found the peace and quiet he longed for. He doubted if he ever would find it this side of the grave. What they did to him then would not matter.

The weariness of despair seeped through him and he fell asleep in his clothes, the door still unlocked. But no one came in. He was not disturbed by any noise in the hushed waiting town, and he slept through the rest of the day, waking up late in the afternoon irritated with himself for his carelessness and in a bad mood in general. His feet had swollen in his tight boots and that did not help. He was almost startled when he glanced in the bureau mirror and saw the cold glitter in his gray eyes that was accentuated by the scowling dark brows. As he went down the stairs he hoped no one would rile him. He was not in the mood to avoid trouble.

Sam Dauber was not at the desk, but Graben found Jill Dauber in the dining room. She had heard him tramping down the stairs and was waiting for him. But he noticed that although the light was fading from the room, she had not lit any of the candles on the oilcloth-covered tables. Perhaps she thought he would prefer the growing dimness. In case someone decided to take a shot at him through the window, he would be harder to hit in a dark room.

She gave him a searching glance when he came in as if to see what kind of mood he was in, and when she saw the look on his face her eyes became uneasy, even a little apprehensive. Her tone was cautious as she asked, "You weren't hungry at lunch?"

He took a seat at the table where he had eaten before, and where he could keep an eye on the street without outlining himself in the window. "I went to sleep," he said.

"I thought that might have been it," she said. "I thought about calling you, but I wasn't sure you'd want to be bothered." When he made no reply, she said in a different tone, "You better be careful. Some of the Star hands rode in a little while ago. They're in the saloon."

Showing no particular interest, he asked, "Where's Dauber?"

She glanced uneasily toward the door to the lobby. "He's at the saloon too, unless he's sneaked back in without me hearing him. Sometimes he does when he's drinking. He knows I don't like for him to drink." Then she asked, "What would you like to eat? It's a little earlier than we usually start serving supper, but I don't guess it matters."

"Whatever's handy," he said. "Just plenty of it."

"And black coffee?"

He nodded and she went into the kitchen. Left alone, Graben turned his attention to the street. He saw Barney Ludlow tramp by glaring at the dining room window with hard eyes, and turn into the restaurant across the street. A light appeared briefly in the general store, then went out. Hiram Goodman had lit the lamp and then decided he wanted to watch the darkening street without being seen himself. Perhaps he was keeping an eye on the hotel, watching to see if Graben left—perhaps even hoping for a glimpse of Jill Dauber.

Graben started to light one of Hiram's cigars, then changed his mind. There was no point in tempting fate—and it was even possible that Goodman was the one who had fired that shot at him, although Graben could not quite picture the short little storekeeper in a dark alley with a rifle in his hands.

Jill Dauber returned from the kitchen with his food and coffee, set it before him and said, "It's getting a little dark in here. You want me to light the candle, or would you rather I didn't?"

He glanced through the window at the street. "I'd just as soon you didn't."

"Whatever you say." She remained near the table, also watching the street. A breath of cold air found its way into the room, stirring the curtains, and she shivered, folding her arms under her attractive breasts. "It's going to be a cold night," she said. "If you need

more cover, there's some in the hall closet. Or I could get it for you."
She met his glance for a moment. "It gets cold on that second floor.
There's no heat up there."

Was she again trying to tell him something? He looked down at
his plate without seeing it. He had lost interest in her as a woman
and regretted that he could no longer think of her as the impeccable
lady she had seemed at first. It never took him long, he thought wry-
ly, to discover the flaws and weaknesses in people. He had a special
talent for it.

Sam Dauber appeared silently from the lobby—and Graben suddenly remembered the breath of cold air that should have registered
on his awareness immediately. Dauber was not quite steady on his
feet and his red-rimmed eyes showed the dislike and distrust that he
probably would have concealed if he had been sober, out of fear if for
no other reason. He looked at the heaping plate of food before Graben
and then said bitterly to his wife, "It's too early to start serving supper. We don't serve supper here until—hic—six o'clock."

"It will soon be six," she said. "And you know I often start serving
a little early if there's anyone here."

Dauber hiccupped and wiped his mouth with an unsteady hand.
"Well, we don't break the rules for him," he said. "He can wait till six
like everybody else. Not that anybody else is likely to come while he's
here. Not unless they've got a rope with them."

Graben continued eating in silence, watching Dauber with a hint
of cold amusement in his gray eyes, a hint of the indifferent contempt
he felt for the man.

Dauber glared at him with bitter eyes and yelled, "I want you out
of my hotel, you hear! And if you don't leave, I aim to see that something's done about it!"

Having made his threat, Dauber turned and pushed his way out
of the room as if in flight from the possible consequences, looking
back over his shoulder with scared eyes.

Jill Dauber looked at Graben in alarm, as though dreading what
he might do. But he quietly continued his meal with a cold humorless
smile on his hard face.

"It might be better if you did leave," she murmured. "When he
gets like this, there's no telling what he might do."

Graben still did not say anything. He seemed lost in thought,
smiling faintly to himself. But it was a wry, somehow bitter smile.

Jill Dauber watched him anxiously for a few moments, but he

seemed unaware of her presence and she went into the kitchen with a faint dampness in her eyes. When she returned a little later with the coffeepot he had already finished his meal and left the room.

Leaving the hotel, Graben paused on the boardwalk and glanced along the street. His cold eyes rested for a moment on the four horses tied at the saloon rail, then his attention drifted to the dark general store across the street. He felt certain that Hiram Goodman was in the store watching him through the window, and the thought irritated him. He suddenly stepped off the boardwalk and crossed the street to the store. As he shoved the door open he heard a startled gasp and saw the shadowy figure of the storekeeper scurrying toward him.

"You can't come in here!" Goodman cried. "I was just going to lock up!"

"Sure you were," Graben told him, "when you saw me coming."

Goodman peered up at him through the rimless spectacles. His voice was frightened. "What do you want?"

"I don't like your cigars," Graben said, thrusting them into his hand. "I think I'll try a different brand. Don't you keep any Mexican cigars here?"

"See here, you can't bust in here like this!" Goodman said in a tone of outrage. "I'll call the Star hands! They're just over at the saloon!"

"Call them," Graben said and stepped over to the shelf where the cigars were. In the fading light he could just make out the labels on the boxes and he helped himself to a handful of Cubans, then thrust a sack of Bull Durham and some papers in his coat pocket.

"What are you doing?" Goodman cried. "You can't come in here and take whatever you want without paying! I'll send for the sheriff at Socorro! He'll send a deputy to arrest you! Or come himself!"

"You won't send for anyone," Graben said calmly. "Whitey Barlow might not like it. He don't want the law poking around here any more than you do."

"What's that supposed to mean?"

"I thought your face looked familiar and I just remembered where I saw it," Graben said, biting off the end of a cigar and looking through the open door at the street. "It was in a newspaper eight or ten years back. You worked in a bank somewhere back East—at the moment I forget where it was. But there was an investigation into missing funds and you turned up missing. Your name wasn't Goodman then. It was Peabody."

"This is preposterous!" the storekeeper cried hoarsely. "Me, an embezzler!"

"That's the word I was trying to think of," Graben said, still look-ing out at the street. He did not light the cigar. "I wonder what the other men in this town are wanted for."

"As far as I know they're not wanted for anything!" the store-keeper cried. "Neither am I!"

Graben gave him a savage grin and opened his mouth to speak. But the storekeeper stopped up his ears. "I won't listen to any more of your lies!"

"Sure you will," Graben said with confidence. "So will the people of this town. They'll be only too happy to hear all about it."

The storekeeper groaned at the thought.

"Now do you want to call the Star hands?" Graben asked.

Goodman opened his eyes wide and stared indignantly at him. "So that's your game! You intend to blackmail me by threatening to spread these filthy lies about me!"

Graben held out his hand, palm up. "Five hundred dollars and I won't say anything about it. Otherwise *I'll* go to the sheriff."

"But I haven't got five hundred dollars!" the storekeeper cried hoarsely.

"Sure you have. All that money you embezzled from the bank."

"But I never embezzled money from any bank!"

"Don't try to convince me," Graben said. "Try to convince the peo-ple of this town."

The little storekeeper with the huge head and thick glasses groaned and whimpered and wrung his hands.

"Make up your mind," Graben said. "I ain't got all night."

With considerable effort Goodman managed to calm down. "Give me a few minutes," he said. "Wait outside."

"I'll wait here."

The storekeeper's glasses gleamed with hatred in the dark. But after a moment he went around behind the counter and Graben heard him unlocking a safe. "You better not try dragging out a gun," Graben told him, "unless you know how to use it."

"I'm not a killer," Goodman said stiffly. "Or an embezzler either."

Graben grinned and kept his eyes on the street, watching the horses in front of the saloon. He heard the storekeeper muttering to himself as he tried to count the money in the dark. "Hurry it up, Pea-body," he said over his shoulder. "I ain't got all night."

"Goodman!" the storekeeper said in an indignant tone. "The name is Goodman! Try to remember that!"

"Sure," Graben said easily. "Whatever you say. Your secret is safe with me, as soon as I get my hands on that five hundred dollars."

The storekeeper groaned and cussed under his breath. After a moment he came around the end of the counter and reluctantly handed Graben the money. "I hope you realize what you've done," he said bitterly. "Part of that isn't mine. I'm sort of the local banker."

Graben sadly shook his head. "If the people only knew the kind of man they're trusting with their money," he said. "If they knew you've used their money to cover up past crimes."

"You wouldn't dare!" the storekeeper gasped. "There's a limit even the likes of you won't cross! If those people find out what you've done, they'll come after you with a rope!"

Graben smiled as he pocketed the money. "Well, I guess we'll hang together then—won't we, Peabody?"

The storekeeper trembled with rage and indignation. "Goodman!" he said. "The name is Goodman!"

Graben pulled his hat lower over his eyes and looked out at the dark street. "Well, Goodman, I hope the five hundred's all there," he said, "because if it ain't, I'll be back after the rest of it."

He nodded and stepped out into the cold windy street, just as the Star riders left the saloon.

Chapter 7

The four Star hands saw Graben crossing the street and they stopped in front of the saloon to watch him. He saw one of them—a short bowlegged puncher—grinning with savage anticipation. The watchful silence of the other three was like a warning. He spotted the rough-faced, black-bearded Graf among them. Graf was not as tall as he had appeared in the saddle. He was shorter by half a head than one of the others, a lean rangy man wearing a wide-brimmed hat.

Graf said something, not looking at Graben, and then the stubby little puncher with the tough grin called, "Hey, you!"

Ignoring him, Graben kept walking toward the hotel.

"I'm talkin' to you, mister!" the puncher yelled, and ran along the street to head Graben off before he reached the hotel steps. The other three followed at a more cautious and dignified walk.

Graben stopped in front of the hotel and faced the short grinning puncher, who slowed to a stop about ten feet away, his breathing a little irregular from his exertion. The puncher's brown-stubbled face was taut with excitement and the eyes peering at Graben were a little uncertain, even a little scared, as if he regretted his rashness now that he had a closer look at the man he had challenged. The other three halted a little distance behind him and to one side, out of the line of fire, and stood watching in dark wooden-faced silence.

For a full minute Graben stood there, straight and tall and seemingly relaxed, and waited for the stubby puncher to make his play.

But the short man appeared to have lost the power to speak or move. Only his eyes remained active, worriedly watching Graben's right hand and searching for the place where he had his gun hidden. By then it must have seemed obvious even to his friends that Shorty's nerve had failed him. And Graben suddenly turned without a word and went on into the hotel, leaving silence behind him.

Jill Dauber stood just inside the dining room door, watching and listening, her face pale. She looked at Graben with anxious eyes. But he went past her without speaking or even looking at her, and climbed the stairs to his room. He left the door open and stepped over to the window in the dark, looking down into the street.

The four Star hands now stood on the street in a little group, talking softly. As Graben watched, Shorty left the others and went down the street toward the saloon, returning a minute later with a rifle he had no doubt taken from a saddle scabbard. He gave his friends a taut grin and turned toward a dark shack across the street that Graben thought was abandoned. It stood between the barbershop and the general store. Shorty opened the shack door and disappeared inside. The other three stood watching the shack for a few moments and then went back down the street to the saloon.

A cold rage began to stir in Graben. He now considered it very possible, even probable, that Shorty had remained behind last night after the others left, or had doubled back, and taken that shot at him. But if so it had not been without Whitey Barlow's consent and the knowledge of the others. Kate Barlow must have also known about it. She must have known about it when Graben had seen her this morning, despite her superior, self-righteous air.

Moving quickly and silently in the dark, Graben hid the five hundred dollars under a loose corner of the ill-fitting carpet where it curled up against the wall. Then he got the Smith & Wesson .44 Russians out of his saddlebag and belted them on, tying down the holsters. He checked the guns by feel, then left the room and went silently along the carpeted hall to the back stairs. The stairs creaked under his weight, but since the frame hotel was creaking in the wind anyway it was doubtful if a little more creaking would be noticed. He let himself out the back door, looked carefully in every direction, then headed out into the open desert to make a wide circle around the town. He circled to the north, avoiding the lower end of town where the horses in the livery corral might give him away.

Out on the desert, tumbleweeds drifted before the wind like migrating herds of wild animals. The mountains in the distance were dim and hazy, obscured by the blowing dust. Graben, his eyes slitted to keep out the dust, moved quickly from one clump of brush to the next, keeping low to lessen the risk of being spotted. He did not pause until he reached the Star Ranch road north of town, a good two hundred yards from the last building. Then he crouched behind a bush at the edge of the road and looked down the road toward town.

He saw one of the Star riders leave the saloon and swagger along the street. The man stopped in front of the hotel, threw his head back to stare up at Graben's window and shouted, "Come on out, Graben! I dare you! You can't buffalo me like you did Shorty!"

In the dark shack, Shorty's face must have been getting red with resentment. Yet he no doubt knew what the other puncher's game was, just as Graben did. They had got tired of waiting and the man in the street was trying to lure Graben out of the hotel where Shorty could get a shot at him with his rifle.

After a moment Graben crossed the dark road and began circling through the brush toward the rear of the shack where Shorty was. The man in the street kept yelling for Graben to come out and fight, so evidently Graben had not been seen crossing the road.

In the saloon Graf Stoker, the black-bearded Star foreman, poured himself a drink and said with a sneer in his rough arrogant voice, "Hell, he's scared. I think he was even scared of Shorty."

In the hotel dining room the Daubers were eating alone, or Sam Dauber was eating while Jill listened to the lusty boasting of Carl Rodney out in the street. Jill had once thought she was in love with the tall handsome Star rider, who was always smiling and joking, but that small secret longing had died when it became obvious that Kate Barlow, much younger and more beautiful, was also making eyes at the handsome devil. Now Jill found herself making the same mistake with this handsome stranger, Frank Graben—and she had already seen the way he looked at Kate, the way every man looked at her.

Sam Dauber looked at his wife with a sneering, malicious smile. "Where's your hero now?" he asked. "Up there hiding in his room, that's where. He's scared to go out and face Carl Rodney."

Jill's face was pale, her eyes dark with worry. She remained silent, listening to Rodney's jeering voice as he taunted Graben and dared him to come out and fight. She could not see Rodney through the window, but she could see him in her mind—a tall easy-moving man with pale hair and hazel eyes in a face burned a golden brown by the sun. Jill wondered if Carl knew about the words exchanged that morning between Graben and Kate Barlow.

In the meantime Graben had completed his half circle around the northern half of town. Making no sound that could be heard above the wind rattling the dry brush and the loose boards of the frame buildings, he came up to the rear of the shack and looked through cold eyes at the badly warped plank door. The rear windows had been boarded up, so he wasted no time with them. The shack was small, containing only one room, and much shorter than the general store to Graben's left or even the barbershop which had living quarters in the rear. He ignored the barbershop and cast only a brief glance at the one small high window that he could see in the long blank wall of the general store. Then with a gun in his hand he stepped up to the shack door, raised his right boot and kicked the door open.

At the front end of the room he saw a crouching figure whirl toward him. He lifted the Russian pistol and fired three rapid shots, the explosions filling the shack like thunder. The man at the other end of the room crashed to the floor and Graben ducked back outside and ran along the short narrow alleyway to the street.

The tall lean-hipped man who had stood in the street yelling taunts at Graben's hotel window was now walking back down the street toward the saloon and glancing uneasily over his shoulder at the shack.

Graben stepped out to the edge of the street with the smoking gun in his hand and called, "Hey, you!"

The rangy man stopped in his tracks, his right hand hovering over the butt of his holstered gun. Then he slowly turned.

Graben stepped out into the street and holstered his own gun. "You wanted me to come out and fight," he said. "Well, here I am."

The lanky fellow stood frozen in his tracks, silently watching Graben from beneath the wide brim of his hat. Behind him Graf and the other man stepped out of the saloon and the black-bearded Graf said in his hard voice, "Kill the bastard, Carl. You can do it."

Carl spread his left hand in an innocent gesture and started to turn toward the voice, then spun back around and jerked out his gun.

One of the Russians leapt into Graben's fist and exploded. The bullet punched Carl in the gut like a fist and he doubled over, but held onto his gun and tried to bring it up. The Russian barked again and this time Carl wilted to the dust with a bullet in his brain.

Graben strode forward with the gun in his fist and passed the dead man without a glance at the sprawled body. His cold glittering eyes and the gleaming pistol were aimed at Graf and the other man. They stood motionless, watching him approach, their faces hidden in the shadows of their hat brims.

Graben halted ten steps away and said to Graf, "What were you saying a minute ago?" Graf did not answer and Graben snarled through his teeth, "I believe you told him to kill the bastard. Would you like to try killing the bastard?"

Graf stood with his big hands clenched at his sides, the other man motionless beside him. Then Graf's chest rose and fell. He let out a long breath and said heavily, "You've killed two of Whitey Barlow's men, if you got Shorty— "

"I got Shorty."

"I hope you know what that means," Graf said.

"You tell me."

"It means war," Graf said in his deep, heavy voice. "Whitey Barlow will hunt you down."

Graben nodded. "That's what I figgered. And if I'm any judge of men, he won't be alone."

"He won't be alone," Graf agreed. "Every hand he's got will be ridin' with him, and if that ain't enough he'll get more."

"In that case," Graben said, cocking the hammer of the Russian, "I don't guess there's any reason why I shouldn't plug you two here and now, is there? Whittle down the odds a little."

Graf and the other man watched him carefully from the shadows of their hat brims. Neither said anything or so much as moved a muscle.

Graben bared his teeth in a savage grin and eased the hammer down on the Russian. "Get out of here," he said. "And take that carrion with you."

Graf stiffened and his bearded face hardened with anger. Used to giving orders himself, he did not like to take them from anyone except Whitey Barlow. And this stranger's rude, contemptuous manner was almost more than he could swallow. But then he looked narrowly at the gun in Graben's hand and said to the other man, "Come on."

Graben holstered his gun and moved aside to the corner of the nearest building. From there he silently watched while they loaded Carl and Shorty across their saddles and then rode slowly out of town leading the horses of the two dead men.

Only then did he become aware of the utter silence of the town, and he ran an uneasy eye along the deserted street. All the buildings were dark except for the hotel and the saloon, but he knew the town was not asleep. If he did not miss his guess, most of the townspeople were crouched behind dark windows, watching and listening to see if the trouble was over for tonight. The same thought was in Graben's mind. He now felt reasonably sure that Shorty had fired that shot at him last night, but Shorty had not been his only enemy and he was by no means certain that the danger was over, even temporarily.

He carefully reloaded his gun while his eyes continued to watch the shadows and the dark windows across the street. He dropped the gun back into the holster and remained there a while longer with his shoulder against the corner of the building, his hat pulled low over his eyes. Then he moved silently through the shadows to the swing doors of the saloon and stepped inside, adjusting his hat as he strolled casually to the bar.

Max Rumford reluctantly uncorked a bottle and poured him a drink, watching him through sleepy bloodshot eyes. "You've played hell now," he growled, not without a trace of malicious satisfaction. "They won't ever stop now till they get you. Everybody around here liked Carl Rodney." After a moment he added, "And I'm pretty sure Jill Dauber and Kate Barlow were both in love with him."

Graben kept his face blank as he sipped his whiskey, trying not to think about Kate Barlow. "I thought you said Jill Dauber only picked on strangers."

The saloonkeeper raised his bushy gray brows. "Carl Rodney was a stranger when he came here. He stayed at the hotel for about a week before he went out to the Star Ranch to see about a job."

"He one of the ones who joked about her?" Graben asked, studying his drink.

"If you knew Carl Rodney you wouldn't need to ask," the big man growled. "He joked and bragged about everything."

"I guess that answers my question," Graben said. He looked bleakly at his bony weathered face in the back-bar mirror, and then asked, "How many men has Whitey Barlow got riding for him?"

"About ten right now. But he'll hire more when he needs them."

"Gunhands?"

"I wouldn't call them gunhands, exactly. But Whitey Barlow wouldn't keep a man on his payroll who ain't willing and able to use a gun." After a moment he scowled and added, "But I don't reckon they're in your class. Carl Rodney was supposed to be better with a gun than any of the others, and he wasn't fast enough to take you."

"The fast ones don't worry me," Graben said dryly. "It's the slow ones who worry me. They hide in dark buildings with rifles." Then he asked, "You think it was Shorty took that shot at me last night?"

The saloonkeeper regarded him thoughtfully for a long moment, then shook his head. "I don't much think so. Them boys all seemed mighty surprised and tickled about it when I told them."

"Tickled maybe, but not surprised," Graben said. "I told Kate Barlow about it this morning."

"I don't think they'd seen Kate since then," Rumford said slowly. "They left the ranch about sunup this morning and rode over to look in on that squatter and check for signs of rustling over west of here."

Graben's forehead creased in thought and he glanced uneasily toward the swing doors. If what Rumford had said was true, then the man who had shot at him the night before was still alive and might be out there somewhere waiting to take another shot at him as he left the saloon.

"Is there a back door here?" he asked.

Rumford shook his head. "Sorry. Anybody comes here has to use the front door. I don't allow no traffic through my bedroom."

"I can't blame you for that," Graben said. "I'd feel the same way."

The saloonkeeper studied him thoughtfully for a time. "How long you figger you'll last? Just you against about a dozen of them. Not to mention some people here in town who'd like to see you dead."

Graben shrugged and said with callous indifference, "Hell, it's been just me against the world for as long as I can remember. I probably won't last much longer, but the mood I'm in right now I plan to take as many with me as I can. And I don't much care if they see themselves as fine upstanding citizens. I've seen how lowdown mean people like that can be when they think they've got numbers or popular support on their side." He finished his drink and laid some change on the bar. "Well, all I can say is they better stay out of my way from now on. If they won't let me live in peace then I'll die fighting, but I won't be the only one."

He started toward the door, and Max Rumford said, "Hey." Graben looked around and the big man motioned with his head. "Go out the back way. I got no use for you and I'll shed no tears when they bury you. But I've got even less use for cowards and back-shooters."

For a long moment Graben seemed on the point of declining the offer. But then he grinned and headed for the back door. "Thanks."

"Don't mention it," Rumford said after he was gone. The big man reached under the bar for the sawed-off shotgun, broke the gun open and checked the loads, then returned the gun to its convenient place, wondering how soon he would need it. He and two others had cut cards to see which one should try for Graben first. If the first man failed to get him, it would be Rumford's turn next. Now he wished he had stayed out of it, and he hoped the first man would get Graben. But why, he wondered, had he told Graben to use to the back door, when he strongly suspected that the first man was again waiting for him to come out the front?

It was near closing when the first man came in cautiously through the batwing doors. Rumford poured him a drink and asked, "Where's your rifle?"

"Left it in the alley," the man grunted. He frowned at the saloon-keeper. "How did he get out of here without me seeing him?"

"Went out the back way," Rumford said. "I didn't figger you'd be prowling around again tonight, after all that excitement earlier."

"You shouldn't have helped him, Max. Whose side are you on anyway?"

Rumford glanced toward the swing doors. "I've been thinking," he said. "Maybe we should call this thing off and let Whitey's men take care of him. Just keep out of it ourselves."

"We can't do that now, Max," the other man complained. "We all agreed not to chicken out, no matter what. We all swore an oath, remember? And I want your word now that if Graben gets me, you won't let him get away with it."

Rumford shrugged. "You've got my word. If it goes that far, of course there can't be any turning back. I thought that was understood."

The other man drained his glass and wiped his mouth. "I just wanted to make sure, Max. I knew I could count on you. After all," he added, "it ain't like we hadn't done it before."

The saloonkeeper nodded absently. He seemed lost in thought. Presently he stirred and said, "Why do you think he came here in the first place? Think there's any chance he knows about us?"

"How could he, Max? It's been nearly ten years since we hit that bank. But there ain't no sense takin' chances, like I've said all along." In spite of the cold the man took out a handkerchief with an unsteady hand and wiped his sweaty face. "And we better get him as soon as we can, Max, before he gets a chance to talk to anyone, just in case."

Rumford studied the man with sharp eyes. "You all right?"

"Sure, Max. I'll be okay. You know you can count on me to hold up my end."

"We're all getting too old for this sort of thing," the saloonkeeper grumbled. "I'll sure be glad when it's over. I don't reckon any of us will get much sleep till Frank Graben is laid out for burying."

Lying awake in her room, Jill Dauber thought she heard the back stairs creak. She listened, but heard no further sound. Just the wind playing its lonesome music around the hotel. It had wailed through the empty years behind her, and would no doubt wail on through the empty years ahead.

She became aware of the slow, steady beating of her heart, but it was all that moved in her. She felt strangely numb. She kept thinking about Carl Rodney, a man she had lost to a younger and more attractive woman. Now he was dead, killed by another stranger whom she had been on the point of losing her head over, and who would soon be gone if he was not already. From the start she had sensed that this one was beyond her reach, yet for a little while he had seemed drawn to her and that had led her to hope for what could never be.

And in a way she had seen him as her last hope. There had been several others before him, and each time she had hoped that the man would take her with him when he left. And even after the man left without her, she had always told herself that it would be different the next time. But now it was getting too late to keep hoping for the next time. She was running out of time. She would soon be forty, and the time was fast approaching when she would not be able to make any man believe that she was thirty-five or thirty-seven.

She sighed bitterly at the thought that she would probably end up running off one day with old Hiram Goodman, who was always watching the hotel in the hope of catching a glimpse of her, and sneaking over when he thought she was alone. Always spying on her, he had found out about Carl Rodney and some of the others, and had tried to blackmail her with the knowledge. When that had not worked, he had begged her to go away with him, saying he would just leave the store and everything behind, if only he could have her. It would have to be him, she thought, the one man she detested above all others, unless it was the one she had married, a sniveling weakling who could no longer make love to her and blamed her for that.

There was only a hint of gray at the window when she heard the muffled and somehow ominous sound of a number of horses walking along the street. She heard the sound for only a moment and then there was silence, a silence even more ominous than the stealthy approach of a group of riders at this hour. She knew they had dismounted and left their horses to close in on foot. She wanted to warn him but she knew it was already too late. She would only give herself away to his enemies.

A moment later she heard the scuff of boots in the lobby and on the stairs, front and back. Suddenly a door crashed open upstairs and she gave a start, he heart in her throat. But the expected roar of gunshots did not follow. Boots pounded back down the stairs and Graf Stoker bellowed angrily, "The bastard ain't here! He's gone!"

Chapter 8

Riding down out of the hills that morning, Rube Cushing and his men saw the smoke when they were about a mile from their shack. After some debate they cautiously rode toward it, called a hello and got no reply. They walked their horses closer and peered with interest at the small fire and at the rocks and trees around it, but saw no sign of anyone.

"That's odd," Cushing said, patting his pockets for smoking material and finding none. "Looks like he just went off and left his fire burnin', whoever it was."

"He must still be around here someplace," muttered Pete Lutter, a tall gawky fellow with small mean dark eyes and a long narrow face. "Nobody but a fool would go off and leave a fire burnin', and a fool never would of got this far in this country."

"I don't know," Rube Cushing said, glancing benignly at the puzzled faces around him. "There's exceptions to ever' rule." They all nodded wisely, and he muttered under his breath, "Dumb sons of bitches. Ain't even got brains enough to know when they're bein' insulted."

Just then a quiet voice said behind them, "You boys looking for someone?"

The heads of Cushing's four men twisted around as if they had been stabbed in the back and the wild looks in their eyes suggested fear that they might be stabbed harder the next time. Cushing himself took his time and he allowed no change to disturb his bland smiling round face, either before or after he recognized the tall dark stranger. Graben stood there beside a big rock casually rolling a smoke while he watched them through slitted gray eyes.

"I had a hunch it would be you," Cushing said with a broad grin. "I was just about to tell the boys here I bet it was you."

"Sure you were," Graben said easily. He licked his cigarette, stuck it in his mouth, lit it and glanced at the other four with a rare tolerance in his bleak eyes. He could see at a glance that they were not too bright, with the possible exception of the one with the sly grin, whose face would have been almost handsome if it had not been for an oddly twisted look, caused perhaps by some missing teeth on one side. That one would bear watching, he thought. They would all bear watching, when it came to that. Being stupid did not prevent them from being mean and treacherous, like most of their kind.

"You decided to pay us a visit?" Cushing asked, still smiling.

"Looks like it was the other way around," Graben said dryly, taking the cigarette from his mouth with his left hand and blowing out a little cloud of smoke. The thumb of his right hand was hooked in his belt near the butt of the birdshead Colt. He was not wearing the heavy Russians. He did not figure he would need them. "Fact is," he added, "I was about to ride on when I heard you boys coming. You always make so much noise?"

Rube Cushing chuckled. Lum Mulock bared his yellow teeth in a stupid grin. The fellow with the twisted face watched him with one eye almost closed. Pete Lutter scowled darkly. The towheaded boy blinked his watery blue eyes in perplexity, as if he could not decide what to make of the grim stranger.

"Hell, I thought we were bein' mighty quiet, for us," Cushing said placidly. "How far back would you say we was when you first heard us?"

"About half a mile, I'd say."

Pete Lutter snorted. "I couldn't hear nobody comin' that far with my ears."

"I wasn't listening with your ears," Graben said.

Rube Cushing chuckled again, but continued to study Graben carefully. "You ain't lettin' them run you out, are you?" When he saw the cold gleam in the slitted gray eyes, he quickly added, "I was hopin' you'd throw in with us. It would give you a chance to get back at them for the way they treated you."

Graben did not say anything. He had already been thinking about that. He had been thinking about it even before Cushing and his men had ridden up. That was why he had built the fire here in broad daylight where they would almost certainly spot the smoke.

For a time he stood there beside the rock smoking his cigarette in silence, looking off toward the east with his bleak gray eyes.

"What do you say?" Cushing asked finally.

"I'm thinking it over," Graben said, and smoked a while longer, handling the cigarette with his left hand, his right remaining near the birdshead Colt in his waistband. He was wearing the short black corduroy jacket and it was unbuttoned, the butt of the gun plainly visible. For a time his leathery face remained blank and unreadable, but then it began to get increasingly hard and grim, the narrow gray eyes glittered like ice, and Cushing's men shifted uneasily in their saddles. But Graben seemed unaware of their existence. His thoughts were elsewhere.

Then he dropped the cigarette, carefully stepped on it, and said as if to himself, "Being honest and reliable and trying to give everybody a fair shake has never done me a bit of good. Well, from now on they can take their chances."

He disappeared behind the rock and reappeared a moment later leading the blue roan. He kicked dirt over the small fire and stepped into the saddle. He barely glanced at the others, but squinted thoughtfully at the fat outlaw chief. "You sure you know what you're getting into?" he asked. "I left a couple of dead men back in town."

"Oh?" Cushing said with interest. "You happen to catch their names?"

"Somebody mentioned Carl and Shorty."

Cushing blinked at him in surprise. "Carl Rodney?"

Graben nodded. "I believe so."

Cushing glanced at the astonished faces of his men and began to grin. "Whitey Barlow ain't goin' to like you killin' off his top gunhand. You sure it was Rodney?"

"It was Rodney all right."

"How about that," Cushing said. "He was supposed to be the very best old Whitey had with a gun, unless it's that new feller we ain't heard much about. Knell, I think they call him."

"What does he look like?"

"Tall, like you. Looks a lot like you, as a matter of fact, except his eyes are darker. He was wearin' dark clothes when I saw him, and a tied-down gun."

"I think I saw him last night," Graben said. "I couldn't tell much about his face, but the rest of the description matches."

"What did he say?"

"He didn't say anything. Graf Stoker did all the talking."

"That sounds like Knell all right. Stoker too," Cushing said. He thought for a moment, his jolly round face and bright friendly eyes giving him more the look of a happy clown than a notorious outlaw. Then he shrugged. "My invite still goes. If you want to throw in with us, I'd be real pleased to have you. I could use a man like you in my outfit."

He gestured at his men. "Get acquainted with my boys. The beanpole with the mean eyes is Pete Lutter. The chunky one with the stupid grin is Lum Mulock. The skinny one with the sly grin calls hisself Paris France."

"It's my real name too," the man with the twisted face said, grinning.

Cushing chuckled as he indicated the towheaded kid. "And this here young feller claims he's Billy the Kid. So you better watch out for him."

Graben looked at "Billy the Kid" with interest. The young man was about nineteen, with bewildered, watery blue eyes and long crooked yellow teeth now bared in a nervous grin. He appeared to still have most of his baby fat, yet already showed signs of premature aging. His hair was thinning and he was starting a paunch. He was close to six feet tall, almost as tall as Graben.

"You sure have changed," Graben said, deliberately looking him up and down with bright narrow eyes. "Growed some too. Pat Garrett ain't going to like it when he finds out about this."

The Kid's mouth fell open. "Who's Pat Garrett?"

"My, you sure have got a short memory," Graben said. "Pat Garrett's the man who killed you a while back."

"The hell you say! Didn't nobody kill me! I'm still alive!"

"So I see," Graben said, while Cushing and the others chuckled in a way that suggested they had never really believed the awkward, bewildered looking boy was Billy the Kid. "That bullet old Pat put in you seems not to have done you a bit of harm. You're not only still alive, you've grown about four inches taller and gained forty or fifty pounds. I'll have to find out your secret, so when somebody kills me I can come back after the bastard."

Cushing smiled uncomfortably and said, "We better get started." He was again hunting for something to smoke.

Graben drew five cigars from an inside pocket and started to hand them to the fat man, then glanced at the kid and kept one. "Here, you boys divide these up."

Cushing grinned with pleasure. "So long as they're free. I never could resist a bargain."

"How we gonna divide four cigars?" the Kid asked, already sensing who would be left out.

"I figgered you were too young to smoke," Graben said, biting off the end of the one he had kept. "It might stunt your growth. But I reckon there ain't much danger of that. If a bullet didn't stunt it, a cigar probably wouldn't. Next time I'll try to remember to bring you one."

The others laughed cheerfully, for by then the cigars had been passed around and only the Kid had not received one, as expected. He watched resentfully as they lit up and puffed their cigars with exaggerated enjoyment.

"Now I know you ain't Billy the Kid," Graben said. "If you were, you'd be shooting by now."

The boy's face got red, but he did not say anything."

The others were still smiling as they started down through the pinons and junipers, but Pete Lutter's smile faded when Graben fell in beside Cushing in the lead, which seemed natural somehow, at least to Graben. It never occurred to him that anyone in an outfit such as that would question his right to be there.

"Did you know Bonney?" Cushing asked.

Graben shook his head. "I'm pretty sure I saw him once at Lincoln. Seemed like every time I looked around I'd see a bowlegged little squirt off behind me someplace keeping an eye on me. I'm not sure what his game was or what he had in mind, but I started keeping an eye on him and after a while he went on about his business."

Cushing smiled back over his shoulder at the towheaded youth bringing up the rear, then said to Graben, "Our boy couldn't be the real Billy the Kid, then?"

"Not unless he's changed a lot and growed a lot," Graben said. "But maybe that wasn't even Billy the Kid I saw. Maybe both me and Pat Garrett were wrong. But if your boy is Billy the Kid, you don't need me. Just tell everyone around here you've got him working for you, and you probably won't have any more trouble."

Cushing grinned. "I already tried that. It didn't work. Whitey

Barlow's men took one look at him and busted out laughin'. Turned into quite a joke. That's what that boy is, a joke."

"If that was Billy the Kid I saw, he didn't look like much either," Graben said. "They might have laughed if they'd seen him, but I doubt if they would have laughed for very long."

Cushing chuckled. "That's the difference with our boy. He didn't do nothin', and then they knew for sure he wasn't Billy the Kid."

They left the pinons and junipers behind them and descended into the barren rocky foothills where nothing grew but cactus and a few stunted cedars. Below them stretched the almost waterless desert plain across which Graben had come. It was close to fifty miles across, with the town of Hackamore near the center. They seemed to be headed in that general direction, and Graben's watchful gray eyes grew uneasy.

"You mind telling me where we're going?" he asked presently.

Cushing eased his bulk in the saddle. His mild round face never changed. "I thought we'd ride down and say hello to that squatter Wilkins," he said around his cigar. "Some of Barlow's men paid them a visit yesterday and I'd like to find out what they had on their minds."

Graben glanced at him in surprise. "It take all of you to do that?"

Cushing smiled. "No, but none of the boys didn't want to miss it. Wilkins has got a right purty daughter. Besides," he added, carelessly flicking ash from his cigar, "we might run into some of Whitey Barlow's boys."

Molly Wilkins turned out to be a lot prettier than Graben had expected, and not at all like he had expected. She appeared to be about seventeen but already had the body of a woman—and the face of a child, the wide innocent eyes of a child. She also had a lot of red hair, and freckles on her nose. She in no way resembled either her slight, balding father or her stout, slow mother.

She seemed delighted to see the rustlers, but when she looked at Frank Graben she seemed to catch a sudden chill, and stared at him in silence, hugging herself. It gave him an odd feeling, although it was not the first time anyone had looked at him that way. She was not afraid of Cushing and his men, a rough lawless bunch if ever there was one. But when she looked at Frank Graben, a handsome clean-cut man by comparison, her smile vanished and she looked almost ill. It gave him something to think about. Did she sense the coiled deadliness in him? Could she tell somehow that she was looking at a killer—which, he sadly admitted, was what he had become. A killer of men.

Cushing went into the house to talk to Wilkins and to eye the stout Mrs. Wilkins. The others dismounted and began firing their guns at rocks and tin cans, showing off in front of the girl and making fools of themselves. Graben loosened his cinch, filled his canteen at the well and watered his horse, aware that the girl was watching him.

He heard her say in a low voice, "Who is that man?"

It was the grinning Lum Mulock who answered. "Calls hisself Frank Graben. Real tough hombre, to hear him tell it."

"His eyes—they scare me."

So that was it. Being handsome would never do him much good as long as he had those cold, slitted gray eyes that chilled every heart, even those in which he might rather have kindled a fire. Not that he had any particular interest in Molly Wilkins. Not after seeing Kate Barlow.

Then Mulock grinned at him and said, "Hey, Graben, why don't you show us what you can do?" There was a kind of malice in the stout, bullnecked man's grin, and a deliberate challenge. The others stopped shooting at the tin cans and turned expectant faces toward Graben, and he saw the same grinning malice in their eyes, the same challenge.

His bleak, hooded eyes shifted briefly to the girl and he saw her hugging herself and trembling, but whether from the cold wind or something else he could not be sure. "Maybe some other time," he said.

Kate Barlow rode into town about noon and stopped at the hotel for a cup of coffee. She did not eat anything. There was a still, numb look on her face, a cold bitter look in her green eyes, and Jill Dauber realized that her niece had been in love with Carl Rodney, as she had already suspected. She wanted to offer some words of sympathy, but hesitated to do so. If Kate knew about Jill and Carl Rodney, she had never let on. Yet Jill often got the feeling, from the way her niece looked at her, that she knew or at least suspected, and now Jill did not know how any expressions of sympathy from her would be received. So she merely watched the girl through veiled eyes and had little to say, except to relate briefly what had happened at the hotel that morning and then to ask if Whitey and his men had returned to the ranch.

Kate shook her head. "I haven't seen them since they left way before daylight. I guess they're still looking for him. That's one reason I came to town, to find out if anyone's started the graves. If he was going to take all the hands with him, he should have got someone here in town to start on the graves and the boxes. But he never thinks of more than one thing at a time."

There was a little silence. Kate sat looking through the window at the street with a damp chill in her green eyes, her coffee forgotten. "I keep thinking about the way Carl Rodney looked when he was alive, and the way he looks now," she said finally. "And that killer picked a fight with him and shot him down. Carl never had a chance."

Jill remembered the way Carl Rodney had stood in the street and hurled insults up at Graben's window and dared him to come out and fight—while Shorty waited in the dark shack with a rifle to shoot Graben down when he came out of the hotel. But from the look on Kate's face, Jill did not think it would do any good to tell her what had really happened. Kate would not believe her, and even if she did, she would hate Jill for telling her. She didn't want anything to tarnish her memory of Carl Rodney.

Chapter 9

Riding back up into the hills with the rustlers, Graben began to have second thoughts about joining up with such a gang. He had no illusions about such men and he knew he could never be one of them. Not even if he rode with them and rustled with then and did all the things they did. He might share their grub and sleep in the same shack but he would remain a man apart, aloof and alone.

He had known from the start—ever since Cushing had spoken to him in the Last Chance Saloon—that they did not need him to help them steal cows, and he had taken it for granted that Cushing wanted him on their side in an expected fight with Star. The idea had not appealed to Graben until a fight between himself and Star seemed inevitable, and then it had occurred to him that perhaps he could use Cushing and his men just as they planned to use him, as an unpaid gunhand in their private war.

But now Graben was beginning to get a feeling he did not like. He had learned to trust his hunches and now he had a hunch that he had underestimated the fat, slow-moving man with the mild round face and innocent eyes. More and more he doubted if Cushing intended to use him in a fight with Whitey Barlow's outfit. Even with Graben on his side, he stood little chance of winning such a fight, for Barlow could hire all the men he needed, however many it took. No, if Graben did not miss his guess, Cushing had something else in mind for him, though for the life of him he could not imagine what it might be.

He felt himself bristling like a new dog in a pack of wolves who might not be as friendly as they seemed. Pretending to check for a possible loose shoe on the blue roan's off front hoof, he reined aside and dismounted, and when they started out again he was in the rear. That seemed to please Pete Lutter, who resumed his place beside the chief. Whether it pleased Cushing or not Graben did not know, but during the rest of the ride he brought up the rear with the towheaded youth who claimed to be Billy the Kid. Apparently it was not from caution that the Kid always brought up the rear, but because he felt that was where he belonged, and because the others felt that was where he belonged.

Now he looked uncertainly at Graben out of his watery pale blue eyes and bared his yellow teeth in a nervous grin. "I been thinkin' about what you said earlier, about seein' me somewheres. I've prob'ly growed a lot since then, and I reckon that's why you didn't recognize me."

Graben squinted thoughtfully at him. "Yeah, that must be the reason," he said.

Paris France and Lum Mulock were riding just ahead of them, at the center of that small cavalcade winding up the hill trail. Paris France whispered something to the bullnecked rider, and then Mulock turned in his saddle and looked at the birdshead Colt in Graben's waistband. "That the only gun you got?" he asked.

"Not hardly," Graben said.

The rustlers' layout turned out to be not quite what he had expected. The shack of unpeeled logs was on a bench surrounded by the pinon and juniper forest. The pole corral was empty. He saw no sign of the cattle the rustlers were supposed to steal.

Seeing the puzzled look on his face, Cushing said, "We never bring them here. That's why Whitey Barlow and his boys ain't already tried to string us up. If they found cow tracks around here, even if they didn't find any cows, that would be proof enough in their minds."

"What about horses? You must have some extra horses."

"Horses is another matter. We've got some runnin' loose around here somewhere, but they're our own, bought and paid for." The fat man grinned. "The only way Whitey Barlow will ever get the goods on us is to catch us roundin' up some of his stock, and so far he ain't had much luck doin' that. If he hired enough men to cover all the range he claims, just payin' them would break him in no time. So far he's been grittin' his teeth and bidin' his time, waitin' for us to slip up. But he knows he's loosin' stock and he's tired of it. One of these days he's liable to decide to come after us, whether he's got any proof or not."

"Me being here could bring him here that much sooner," Graben said.

Cushing nodded. "I thought about that."

That was all he said on the subject, and it left Graben puzzled as they stripped the gear from the horses, watered them at the small waterhole in a little hollow below the shack and turned them into the corral. If Cushing was trying to avoid a fight with Star, why did he want Graben here, knowing what it could mean?

"Kid, you trot back down the trail a piece and keep a eye peeled," the big man said. "Let us know if you see anyone comin'. Graben, you can toss your roll on that lower bunk in the corner. It's the only one vacant. If you don't like it you might trade with someone. I'll be in there in a few minutes."

Graben saw Cushing and Pete Lutter exchange a silent glance, and Lutter remained near the corral with the fat rustler chief while the Kid trotted back down the trail with his rifle and Graben followed Paris France and Lum Mulock into the shack. He noticed that those two were grinning as usual. They always seemed to be sharing some private joke or plotting some mischief between them.

"There's your bunk, Graben," Paris France said, without looking at him. "You'll find it about as comfortable as the rest, which ain't sayin' much."

Graben tossed his blanket roll and saddlebags on the bunk indicated and then glanced briefly about the shack's one large room. Besides the row of frame bunks along one wall, the only furniture was a long plank table and several homemade chairs. There was no stove, but there was a rock fireplace at the back where the rustlers evidently did their cooking.

Paris France and Lum Mulock stretched out on their bunks, one above the other, and giggled like boys at some joke Graben had missed. He stepped over to the window and looked out, scowling. Cushing and Pete Lutter were still out by the corral with their heads close together. Restless and on edge, Graben suddenly left the shack and strode across the hard-packed ground toward them. They broke off their quiet conversation as he approached, and their blank faces offered no clue to what they had been talking about.

"I reckon you know Whitey Barlow and his men will be dogging

my trail," he said. "It will surprise me if they don't show up here before long."

Cushing nodded, his face still blank. "Me and Pete was just talkin'
about that. Why don't you go back and tell Paris and Lum to come
out here. I'm gonna send them back down the trail a piece, so maybe
they can give us a little more advance warnin' if they see Whitey and
his boys comin'."

Graben turned and went back to the shack. At the door he stopped
in his tracks. Lum Mulock sat on Graben's bunk opening his saddlebags while Paris France watched curiously from his own bunk.

"Find anything you like?" Graben asked.

The swarthy fellow looked up at him and bared his ugly teeth in
a grin, showing neither uneasiness nor embarrassment. Mulock was
far too coarse a ruffian for such squeamish sentiments. He chose to
regard the matter as a joke, and his grin dared Graben to do anything about it. "Not yet," he said. "You got back too soon."

For a long moment Graben stared at him in silence with a look
in his icy gray eyes that quite a few men had seen just before they
died. But Mulock stared back at him unafraid—the bullnecked fellow
was perhaps too stupid to be afraid, or too conceited about his own
strength and prowess. And Graben slowly sighed and forced himself
to relax, for as much as he wanted to kill the man, he knew it would
be a mistake to do so. He had more important worries, and too many
enemies without turning the other rustlers against him.

"Better get outside," he said. "Cushing wants you. Both of you."

Mulock shrugged and pushed himself up from Graben's bunk,
leaving the saddlebags open. Paris France got up from his own bunk
and followed him, both of them still grinning as they went out by
Graben, who moved aside to let them pass.

Graben turned to watch through the doorway as they started toward the corral. Then he went over to his bunk to make sure nothing
was missing from his saddlebags. After a slight hesitation he took
out the cartridge belt and holstered revolvers and strapped them on,
tying down the holsters. He felt ready then for whatever happened.

Going over to the window, he watched Mulock and France saddle
up and ride back down the trail the way they had come. A moment
later Pete Lutter threw the rig on his own horse and rode off through
the trees in a different direction, and Cushing turned and waddled
toward the shack, smoking the stub of the cigar Graben had Given
him. When he came in the fat man glanced at the Russian pistols, but

made no comment.

Instead he said, "There ain't much way they can sneak up on us now. I sent Lum and Paris back down the trail to watch the desert, and Pete over to that high peak north of here where he can see for miles." Just walking from the corral had apparently left Cushing a little out of breath, and he looked uncomfortable as he glanced at Graben and added, "If they do spot them, it might be a good idea for you to light out for a while and stay out of sight till they leave. I can tell them you stopped here for a bite to eat and then rode on."

The fat man rubbed his hands together and grinned. "Speakin' of food, why don't we see if we can rustle up a little bite of something while we wait."

It was a long wait, and the waiting soon got on Graben's nerves. He did not like any part of Cushing's plan. None of it made any sense to him, and he began to wonder if the jolly fat man had any brains after all. But it would seem like bad policy to start out by questioning the rustler's judgement.

After he had eaten enough beans and sowbelly for four men, Cushing relit the last inch of his cigar, raked the dishes and crumbs aside and dealt himself a hand of solitaire while Graben restlessly paced the floor. For a time Cushing watched him in silence, seeming to take a great interest in every move he made and to enjoy his obvious uneasiness. More and more Graben felt that he was putting his life in the hands of a jolly fat schemer who stood to profit in some way by his ruin. And the longer he remained here, the less chance he stood of getting away alive.

"I might as well go now," he said finally. "If I wait till they show up, it will be too late to leave."

"Relax," Cushing said with annoying cheerfulness, with that grinning malice Graben had noticed in all the rustlers, unless it was the bewildered looking boy who called himself Billy the Kid. "You're jumpy as a fox in a chicken house."

Graben scowled. "Right now I feel more like one of the chickens."

Cushing chuckled as if he thought that a pretty good joke. His plump hands continued to flip out cards from the deck with irritating regularity while his glowing yellow eyes watched Graben like a spider watching a fly. Common sense should have warned him of approaching trouble, yet there he sat, playing his game of solitaire, apparently relaxed and even enjoying the situation.

The warning signal in Graben was pounding like a drum. The

feeling that something was very wrong here grew into certainty. Without a word he suddenly went over to the bunk in the corner and slung his saddlebags and blanket roll over his shoulder.

"You leavin'?" Cushing asked.

"That's right."

He gave the fat man at the table a cold glance and saw neither surprise nor disappointment in his plump round face. There was even a look of gloating satisfaction in Cushing's eyes, and Graben got the uneasy feeling that even his leaving was part of Cushing's plan, whatever it was.

"That might be best," Cushing said, his voice soft and mild as usual—but a voice Graben could no longer trust. "Clear out till they leave—"

Graben went out without waiting for him to finish. He had heard it before. And if he came back at all it would only be to find out what Cushing's game was—and to put a bullet in him if it turned out that Cushing was trying to double-cross him in some way.

Outside, Graben darted sharp narrow glances at the rocks and brush and scraggly trees on the nearby slopes. In his present frame of mind he half expected a bullet from an unseen gun. But the silence held as he crossed to the corral and saddled the blue roan. He did not once glance back at the shack, for he knew that Cushing was too clever a man to do his own killing, if killing was what he had in mind.

Graben was lashing his blanket roll behind the cantle when he heard a single horse pounding up the trail at a hard run. He swung into the saddle and a moment later Lum Mulock rode his lathered horse into the yard, skidding to a stop when he saw Graben. The chunky bullnecked rider was breathing almost as hard as his horse, but his yellow teeth were bared in the grin Graben was beginning not to like.

"You better hightail it out of here, Graben," he said maliciously. "The whole damn Star outfit is right behind me."

"Where's France?"

"He stayed to ask for a smoke and maybe slow them down a little. But I don't think it worked, 'cause when I was back down there a piece I saw about ten riders closer than where I left him."

Graben listened, and after a moment his ears picked up a faint distant rumbling that he knew was caused by a number of hard-ridden horses coming up the rocky trail. In only a few seconds the sound swelled and became more distinct. He had no time to waste.

As he lifted the reins he glanced at the grinning Mulock and reluctantly nodded his thanks. Of all the rustlers he liked Mulock the least, but the man had punished his horse to warn him, and Graben was not one to overlook a favor, however slight. "Adios," he said.

Mulock shrugged, then pulled his Winchester from the scabbard and tossed it to Graben, saying, "You might need this."

Graben caught the rifle and scowled for a moment, on the point of tossing it back to the swarthy man. Then it occurred to him that if he kept the gun there might be less danger of getting shot in the back as he rode away. So he grunted his thanks, turned the blue roan and headed for the trees. Glancing briefly at the shack, he saw Cushing standing in the door watching him. The fat man waved casually but did not say anything.

Graben turned along a narrow trail and followed it around the hillside through the pinons and junipers. When he had gone a hundred yards a thought occurred to him. He sniffed the breech of the rifle and knew it had been fired only a short time ago. A warning clawed through him that the rifle might also be part of Cushing's plan, and he threw the gun away into the brush and rocks beside the trail.

A few minutes later the trail descended to a narrow open valley. He started to avoid this open stretch, then decided it would be a waste of time, for he believed the danger was still a piece behind him, and it would be best to keep to the trail for now and keep moving as rapidly as possible. Later there would be time to hide his tracks and plan his next move.

He did not know where the shot came from. Later he was never completely sure that he had heard the shot, or felt the bullet. He could not remember falling out of the saddle. The first thing he became vaguely conscious of was that he was lying on the ground. Then he thought he heard boots tramping rapidly toward him, and a moment later hands patted his pockets, unbuckled the cartridge belt and tugged it loose. But all this seemed like a dream, and as in a dream he could not move, despite a warning somewhere in his brain that he was in deadly peril.

Then there was another shot, from somewhere close by. The man bending over him gave an involuntary cry of alarm and scrambled away, and then everything seemed to fade, as if the dream had ended.

When the Star hands rode up with Graf Stoker in the lead, they found the man called Knell standing alone in the little valley, looking down at a spot of blood on the ground.

"Did you see him?" Stoker asked excitedly.

Knell gravely shook his head. "I heard a couple of shots, but when I got here all I found was a spot of blood on the ground. There's tracks leading to here, but none leading away."

"What do you mean?" Stoker cried hoarsely, swinging down from his saddle and striding toward him.

"Look for yourself," Knell said.

The black-bearded foreman did look, scowling darkly. But all he saw was the blood on the ground, and some tracks leading to it, but none leading away—just as Knell had said.

Stoker raised his dark face and glared at one of the men still in the saddle—the one member of the group who did not seem to belong there. "What the hell's goin' on here?" Stoker barked. "You bastards playin' some kind of game?"

"All I know is what I already told you," Paris France said, looking mighty uncomfortable, and just as puzzled as the rest of them. "Graben shot Whitey Barlow and then hightailed it back to the shack. I didn't go back with him because I never had no part in it and I didn't want it to look like I did. So I stayed and waited for you boys, and you heard what Cushing said when we got to the shack. He said Graben rode in fast and told him he'd just killed Whitey Barlow, then switched back to his own horse and lit out headin' this way. That's all I know."

Graf Stoker swept the rocky slope above them with a dark glance. "Well, he's got to be around here someplace. He couldn't of gone far without leavin' a trail. Spread out and start lookin'."

They searched for Graben until after dark, and then began the long ride back to the ranch in somber silence with the dead Whitey Barlow across his saddle. The man called Knell volunteered to stay behind and keep looking, since he never slept much anyway, and he said too that he felt responsible for Graben's escape, since Stoker had sent him to seal off this trail and he had failed to do so.

It was not until two days later that Knell got back to the ranch. Kate Barlow sent for him immediately. He found her seated on the couch in the living room. Her thin lips were pressed together and there was an indescribable bitterness in her green eyes. Her face was drawn and pale and she looked several years older than when he had last seen her only a few days before. She did not ask him to sit down and he remained standing with his black hat in his hand. He was dusty and tired and his dark eyes betrayed how little he had slept.

"Did you see any sign of that man?" she asked.

He sighed and shook his head. "Not a trace."

She studied him for a time with chilly eyes, the rest of her face unreadable. "Some of the hands were back over there yesterday," she said, "and they never found a trace of you either. They couldn't even find your trail."

The faintest suggestion of wry humor touched Knell's dark gray eyes. "I don't want to cast any reflection on those boys, ma'am, but I got the impression that some of them were a lot better at working cattle than at reading sign. But that's hard rocky ground where I was, and I reckon that's one reason none of us managed to find Graben's trail. I made about a dozen circles through those hills, each one wider than the one before, and I never found a single track."

"You think those rustlers could be hiding him?"

Knell thought for a moment, then shook his head. "I don't much think so." He hesitated, then added almost reluctantly, "As a matter of fact, I've got a feeling one of them shot him. They won't admit it because they're afraid he may still be alive and may come back."

Kate Barlow almost smiled. "That's funny," she said. "Graf Stoker said the same thing about you. He said he thought it was you who shot Graben but that you weren't letting on because you were afraid he might come back after whoever did shoot him. He said that was probably the reason why you were trying so hard to make sure he didn't get away."

Knell again shook his head, almost smiling himself, but not quite. "No, it wasn't me," he said. "I'd be willing to bet it was one of Cushing's men."

A frown creased Kate Barlow's forehead. "Why would they try to kill him?"

"I've been wondering about that myself, ma'am," he said slowly. "I've got a notion in my head, but I could be wrong, so I'd better keep it to myself."

Kate Barlow seemed to lose interest in him. For a time she sat lost in thought, the bitterness returning to her green eyes. Then she said as if to herself, "That man has killed the two people who meant most to me, my father and Carl Rodney. But if he's still alive he'll come back after the man who shot him, and when he does we'll be ready."

Knell was silent for a moment. "Has it occurred to you that it might not have been Graben who shot your father?"

"No," she said, "it hasn't occurred to me."

Chapter 10

Standing at the Last Chance bar five months later, smoking his thin cigar, Frank Graben regarded Lum Mulock with a cold narrow glance. It bothered him that he could not remember whether the swarthy, heavyset man had had the mustache before or not. But he remembered the man's ugly yellow teeth and annoying grin well enough.

He also remembered the rifle Mulock had tossed to him just before he had ridden away from the rustler shack—a rifle that had just been fired. "So you think it was me who killed Whitey Barlow?" he asked.

Lum Mulock looked down at his glass and his grin got a little broader. "That's what I heard."

"Who did you hear it from? Your old pal Paris France? Where is he anyway? I thought you two were always together—except for that time when he stayed behind to tell the Star hands it was me who shot Whitey Barlow instead of you."

"I don't know what you're talkin' about, Graben," Mulock said easily, obviously enjoying himself. He seemed too stupid to realize the danger he was in. "Me and Pete Lutter had gone to round up some horses that day. You borrowed my rifle and rode off with Paris. I forget where the Kid was."

"That the story Cushing made up for you to tell everyone?"

"That's how it was, Graben. Gettin' shot must of damaged yore memory. I've heard that happens sometimes."

"My memory's okay," Graben said, although he was still uneasy about Mulock's mustache, and he could not remember much that had happened after he was shot. He had regained consciousness in an old prospector's shack a day's ride to the north and west, with a worried silent doctor from a nearby town working on him. The prospector told him that a man had brought him and left him there—a tall man in black, with a hard face and dark eyes. The man had not given his name, but he had left some money with the prospector, enough to pay for the doctor and Graben's keep until he was back on his feet. Now Graben owed his life to a man whose name he did not know, whose face he would not recognize if he saw it.

Graben's wallet and the money in it had been taken from him by the man who had shot him, as well as his shell belt and holstered Russians. But in his haste the man had overlooked the birdshead Colt in his waistband—and the five hundred dollars in his saddlebag which the man in black had not bothered either. Perhaps the stranger had not known the money was there, but Graben had a feeling that he would not have taken it anyway.

Now Graben had come back to find and kill the man who had tried to kill him. Yet he knew that more than one man had been involved. Quite a few men had tried to bring about his death. They would all have to pay. He was tired of people trying to kill him.

He propped his elbows on the bar and turned sideways, studying Mulock with a puzzled expression in his eyes. Mulock grinned back at him with a bold indifference that amounted almost to a challenge. "You really don't know what's going to happen, do you?" Graben asked.

Mulock laughed. "I know what's gonna happen all right. You're gonna get yourself killed. If somebody here in town don't do it, the Star hands will, when they find out you're back."

"And you find that funny?"

Mulock shrugged. "It will be a change. There ain't been hardly no excitement around here since you left."

"They ain't given you boys any trouble about stealing their beef?"

"Nah," Mulock said and grinned. "Us boys and Star has been plumb cozy ever since we tried to help them get the man that killed their boss. We're even on speakin' terms, more or less. 'Sides, they ain't never been able to prove it was us stealin' their beef. It might be Apaches. Them red devils has been causin' all kinds of trouble over west of here lately. Or it might be greasers sneakin' up from the border."

"It might be," Graben agreed. "But it ain't."

Mulock laughed and bent over his glass. He finished his drink and wiped the back of a rusty-looking hand across his scraggly mustache. "I better be headin' back. Rube and the boys will be real interested to hear you're back."

"Tell them they can expect a little visit from me when they least expect it," Graben said.

Lum Mulock chuckled and went out with his yellow teeth bared in the ever-present grin. Even after he had mounted his horse and ridden out of town his grinning face remained in Graben's mind. It was accompanied by another picture, but one more shadowy—of Graben himself, with a gun in his hand, blasting that hated grin to hell.

He glanced at Max Rumford and found the saloonkeeper glaring at him through bloodshot eyes. "You sure got a talent for making enemies," Rumford growled. "You couldn't even hit it off with them rustlers."

"I didn't try to."

"That's what I figgered. And now there's four or five more people who'll be smiling at your funeral."

"There won't be any funeral."

"I never figgered there would be, for the likes of you," the saloonkeeper said bluntly. "Not in this town. But you know what I meant."

"I know," Graben said and poured himself another drink, his gaunt weathered face reflecting the cold sick feeling in his gut. When it had begun to appear that he might recover from the bushwhacker's bullet, he had hoped that the cold warning of death had been a false alarm. But the coldness was still there and now he knew it would remain there until he died. He was running out of time. For he had a fatal disease. There was something about him that made men hate him and fear him and want to kill him. And every moment brought him that much closer to the one who would succeed.

Rumford was still watching him through those unpleasant, red-hazed eyes. The saloonkeeper did not look like he had slept much lately. "So you came back to get even with everybody for what happened to you," he growled. "Hell, you should of considered yourself lucky and kept going."

Graben gave him an icy look. "Lucky?"

Rumford nodded. "Lucky just to be alive. The next one will prob'ly be fatal. A lot of folks around here ain't going to like you coming back and stirring things up again. They were starting to think we were rid of you, that you'd crawled off someplace and died."

Graben drained his glass and laid his money on the bar. "What did you think?"

"Me? I figgered they were damn fools for thinking that just because it was what they wanted to think, and I told them so."

"Ludlow and Dauber?"

"I ain't naming no names," Rumford said. "But I can tell you right now, they ain't the only enemies you've made in this town. And just so we understand each other, from now on you can go out the way you came in, like everybody else. I've got to live in this town, mister. It's too much trouble to move, and I got nowhere to go."

Graben shrugged. "I figger I'm as apt to get shot going out the back door as the front. That brush out there is a good place for someone to be waiting with a rifle."

Rumford scowled at him. "Course, there's another solution to the problem. You might try to quit drinking. I hear it's bad for your health."

Graben smiled. "That's strange advice from a saloonkeeper. But I appreciate your concern for my health."

Rumford's face heated with anger. "I don't give a damn about your health and you know it," he said. "But if you're determined to get yourself killed, I'd just as soon you did it someplace else. If the sheriff takes a notion to ride over this way, I don't want him asking me a lot of stupid questions."

"I had a feeling you wouldn't like that," Graben said. "I imagine there are quite a few people in this town who'd be just as happy if they never saw the sheriff. There usually is in a place like this."

The saloonkeeper regarded him with a hostility bordering on hatred. "Maybe you'd like to explain that."

"Sure," Graben said readily. "I figger about half of the people in this town came here because they were wanted somewhere else. That's why I don't like it when they try to get so high and mighty with me. I'm not wanted for anything anywhere, as far as I know."

Max Rumford took a deep breath and his voice shook with the effort to control his anger. "You talk about high and mighty. You should take a good look at yourself, mister. But what you said about the people of this town—you could be right. They don't want no lawmen nosing around here, and they don't want you causing no more trouble that might bring them nosing around, asking a lot of questions. If you had any brains you never would of come back here, knowing what to expect."

"What's that?"

The saloonkeeper raised his bushy gray brows. "It's just like Lum Mulock said. You're going to get yourself killed."

Graben shrugged. "If it don't happen here, I figger it will happen somewhere else before long," he said in a quiet, indifferent tone. "That's why I decided to come back. I'd just as soon die here and take as many of you bastards with me as I can."

"That might not be as many as you think," Rumford told him in a low, deadly voice.

"It might be a lot more than you think," Graben replied, and strode from the saloon in time to see the squatter Wilkins coming along the street on his plodding work horse. Wilkins stared at him with bright curious eyes, and for his part Graben had a few questions he wanted to ask the squatter. But just then his attention was diverted by another rider entering town from the north. This horse and rider were as different as could be from Homer Wilkins and his ungainly animal.

It was Kate Barlow on her claybank.

One small part of Graben's mind was aware of the squatter turning in the saddle to watch him as he rode past. But his own eyes remained on Kate Barlow as he strolled on along the boardwalk. He did not miss the change in her when she saw him. She stiffened visibly and then leaned forward in the saddle, peering at him. When she was about forty feet away she stopped her horse in the middle of the street and sat her saddle staring at him with a look of murder in her green eyes. Her thin lips were pressed together over clenched teeth and she was trembling with cold fury and the effort to control herself.

Graben sighed a little when he saw that look of cold hatred on the face of a woman he had never wanted to hurt. That night when he had first seen her in the hotel dining room, with her rosy tan cheeks glowing in the lamplight and the dark hair falling over her graceful shoulders—he had sighed a little even then, thinking how nice it would be to spend the rest of his life with a woman like that. But he had known from the start that such a thing could never be, because of the kind of man he was, and because she was Whitey Barlow's daughter and shared her father's opinion of him. He had also known that he would not try to change her opinion of him or melt the coldness in her heart. It was not in him to try to win the affection, certainly not the love, of someone who hated everything he stood for. Call it pride, call it what you will—that was how he was.

And now he knew it was too late for him to be thinking about a woman like Kate Barlow or any other. That time was past. It had probably already been too late when he had first ridden into this country, but when he had come back it had been with the knowledge that he probably would not leave again. For the time that remained he would be what he had always been, and if possible do what he had set out to do. He would not let Kate Barlow or anyone else stop him if he could help it.

Yet he could not really blame her for feeling as she did about him. It had been inevitable from the start. It was in the cards. And he almost touched his hat in token of admiration for her beauty, for the fine figure she cut on her horse in the sunlight. If he had done so, it would have been a kind of goodbye, not just to her, but to his old dream of a woman like her. But he did not make the gesture, because he knew she would not understand it. She would regard it as a kind of insult. For what he felt did not show on his hard face or in his cold gray eyes. If any of it showed there it was only a faint trace of loneliness that looked more like aloof indifference. He had almost forgotten how to smile. When he did smile it looked more like a sneer.

So he did not smile, or touch his hat, or even nod his head. He just turned his back on her and entered the hotel. As he crossed the lobby on his way to the stairs he could hear the clock on the wall ticking. There was no one at the desk.

In the street, Kate Barlow took several deep breaths, and then she got an iron grip on her emotions and turned her horse toward the general store. At the rail she swung down carefully, as if not quite sure her legs would support her, and went slowly in through the door, her green eyes like ice and a frozen set to her face. Hiram Goodman stood behind the counter, peering at her through his glasses.

"I want to buy a gun," she said.

"A gun!" He darted a glance toward the hotel. "You can't be thinking of going after him yourself, Kate! That's a dangerous man! Why not let your hands take care of him?"

"I want a gun," she repeated, "and I want it now!"

"Well, all right," the storekeeper said nervously. "Whatever you say." He again peered at her through the thick glasses. "What kind of gun?"

"A pistol. I'd prefer a small one, but I want one that will kill a man. And I want it loaded."

When he got to the top of the stairs Graben found the door of his room standing open. He stopped at the door, a slow frown creasing his forehead. Jill Dauber stood at the window with her back to him, looking down at the street. When she heard him she turned and her green-hazel eyes studied him carefully, trying to read the expression on his face.

"I just came in to see what kind of shape this room's in," she said "I haven't been in here lately."

Graben slowly removed his hat, thinking that she looked older, that there was more gray in her hair, more lines in her face. She seemed thinner and paler. "Dauber probably won't like it," he said.

She shrugged. "I've about quit caring what he doesn't like." Then she added, "Was he downstairs?"

"I didn't see him."

"He's probably shut himself up in his room and started drinking again," she said wearily. "He keeps a bottle in there and uses any excuse to start again. As if things weren't bad enough without that."

Graben did not say anything, and she studied his face in silence for a moment. "You seem different," she said finally.

"I'm still the way I've always been," he said. "Just more so."

"No, you've changed. You seem quieter—and more bitter some-how."

His lips twisted in a mockery of a smile. "I didn't know it showed."

"It shows all right," she said. "And it's partly because you got shot, isn't it?"

His dark brows raised slightly. "That might have something to do with it," he agreed. "That, and all the other things that happened when I was here."

"It will probably start all over again," she said. "It was a mistake for you to come back."

"It was a mistake for me to come here in the first place," he said.

"I don't know," she said, watching him. "If you hadn't, we never would have met."

He glanced at her in wonder, not certain what she meant. He did not know what she thought it had amounted to, or would ever amount to, but if she preferred to believe that meeting her was the most important event in his life, it was not in him to disillusion her or rob her of any small consolation. Whatever her failings as a wife and a Christian, he had no doubt that she was a finer woman than many he had known. And if she was not on his side, at least she did not seem to be against him. Which was more than he could say for anyone else in this town.

"I guess I better get back downstairs," she said, turning to look out the window again. "I saw Kate go in the general store. I guess she'll be over here in a minute. Oh, good Lord! She's coming across the street with a gun in her hand!" Jill quickly crossed the room to the door, saying as she went by him, "You stay here. I'll handle this."

"Better be careful," he warned her. "When people like her start fooling with guns, it's usually innocent bystanders who get shot."

But he doubted if there were many innocent bystanders in this town.

Jill went quickly down the stairs without answering. Kate Barlow was just entering the hotel lobby from the street, a gleaming blue pistol in her hand and an icy resolve to use it in her eyes. Jill stopped at the foot of the stairs and stood blocking her way.

"What do you think you're going to do with that thing?" Jill asked.

"Get out of my way," Kate said and kept coming toward her until she was only a few feet away.

"Do you think he's going to stand still and let you shoot him?" Jill asked. "He'll defend himself if you force him to, and you know what that means!"

"I don't care," Kate said. "He's going to pay for what he did."

"Before you make a fool out of yourself, maybe it's time you heard what really happened that night," Jill said. "I don't think anyone's ever told you the straight of it. Carl Rodney stood out in the street and called Graben names and dared him to come out and fight, while Shorty was hiding in that old shack across the street with a rifle, waiting to shoot Graben the minute he stepped out of the hotel."

"I don't believe you," Kate said.

"It's true all the same," Jill told her. "And I've never believed Graben killed your father. We only have the word of a rustler that it was him. If the truth ever comes out, I imagine we'll find out it was one of those rustlers who killed him."

Kate's lips twisted in scorn. "Would you like to know what I think, Aunt Jill? I think you've lost your head over another stranger with a handsome face. And don't look so surprised. I've known about your little affairs with your hotel guests for a long time. Everyone around here knows."

"That doesn't surprise me," Jill said. "But maybe you haven't heard it all. Have you heard the one about Carl Rodney and me?"

"What do you mean?" Kate asked.

Just then Sam Dauber came unsteadily from the small room behind the desk with a half-empty whiskey bottle in his hand and looked at them with bleary eyes. "Oh, don't mind me," he said with a bitter, crooked smile. "I know all about it. Known about it for years." He took a pull at the bottle, belched and wiped his mouth. "What do you think when on here them two weeks Carl Rodney stayed here?"

He took another swig at the bottle and then waved the bottle in the air. "You know what I used to think? I used to think she did it so men would stay here longer and we could make more money, which Lord knows we needed. I actually thought she was doing it to help me. But you know what I think? I think the old bitch just plain enjoys it." He grinned maliciously. "But I don't think she's had no luck with this Graben so far. Keeps finding some excuse to go up to his room, but she don't stay long enough for nothing to happen. I guess he don't encourage her to stay. Hell, maybe he ain't such a bad feller after all, for a killer."

"You're disgusting," Jill Dauber told him. "Why I ever married you I'll never know."

Dauber stared at her with resentment and hatred. They did not see the dampness in Kate Barlow's eyes. They did not see the gun sag in her hand. It was not until she turned and almost ran from the hotel that they became aware of her again. Then she was gone.

CHAPTER 11

Knell found her sitting on a leather-covered sofa in the living room, wearing a green dress that matched her eyes.

"You wanted to see me, ma'am?" he asked, standing awkwardly at the door with his black hat in his hand.

"Yes, I'd like to talk to you a minute," she said and indicated a chair. "Sit down."

"I'd just as soon stand, ma'am. I'm sort of dusty."

"Suit yourself." She studied him curiously for a moment. "I just realized I don't even know your first name."

"It's Mark, but I hardly ever use it," he said. "Everyone who calls me anything calls me Knell."

"That's an odd thing to say."

"I don't know very many people," he said. "Not that well anyway."

She brushed a speck of something from her green dress, and the silky whisper of her fingers on the cloth made a disturbing little sound in the silence. When she glanced up again there was a different expression on her face. "I believe you were in town the night Carl and Shorty were killed, weren't you?"

He answered with a noticeable reluctance. "Yes, ma'am."

"Would you mind telling me exactly what happened that night?"

"Didn't Graf Stoker tell you?" he asked uncomfortably.

She was silent a moment, her face turning red in the lamplight. "I was in town today, and I heard a completely different version of what happened than the one he gave," she said. "I'd like to know the truth. It's very important to me."

He let out a long sigh. "Well, it didn't happen quite the way he said. Shorty first tried to pick a fight with Graben, but he sort of lost his nerve at the last minute and Graben just turned and went on into the hotel without saying anything. Then Shorty got his rifle and went in that old shack by the general store to wait for him to come back out of the hotel, and the rest of us went back to the saloon. But Stoker and Rodney soon got tired of waiting and Rodney went up the street and stood out in front of the hotel and tried to get Graben to come out and fight. But Graben must have seen Shorty go in that old shack with the rifle, and he circled around and kicked the back door open and shot him.

"When Carl realized the trick had backfired, he started back along the street to the saloon. But Graben stepped out of the alley and called to him—"

"What did he say?"

"He said, 'You wanted me to come out and fight. Well, here I am.' About that time Stoker and I stepped out of the saloon and Stoker said, 'Kill the bastard, Carl. You can do it.' Rodney looked like he was going to turn and say something to Stoker, but then he whirled back around and went for his gun. I guess he was trying to catch Graben off guard. But that didn't work either. Graben got his gun out first and killed him."

Kate Barlow sat watching him with the dark shadow of tragedy in her eyes, the still numb look of defeat and despair on her face. "Then it was even worse than Aunt Jill said," she murmured as if to herself. "She didn't tell me the whole story. I never would have thought Carl Rodney would stoop to something like that. Pa tried to warn me that he wasn't any good, but I wouldn't listen." She glanced up at the man called Knell, and behind the long dark lashes her green eyes narrowed slightly in concentration. "Didn't you say once that you didn't think it was Graben who killed Pa?"

"I'm not sure I put it in quite those terms," he said. "But I've never believed he did it. Men like Graben have a certain code. Maybe it doesn't mean much to anyone else, but it means a lot to them. He's the sort of man who prides himself on his skill with a gun. If he'd set out to kill your father, he would have given him a chance to draw. He wouldn't have hid behind a rock and done it with a rifle. He didn't even have a rifle. They claimed he borrowed Lum Mulock's

Winchester, but I figure it was Mulock himself who did the shooting. I imagine Rube Cushing put him up to it. They saw a way to get rid of your father and let Graben take the blame for it. If I'm not mistaken, they then tried to kill Graben to make sure he wouldn't talk, and to get the credit for doing Star a favor. But after he got away, they put their heads together and decided it might not be a good idea to admit shooting him. They knew if he lived he'd be coming back after whoever did it, like I said before."

Kate Barlow studied the tall dark rider carefully while he talked, and then she glanced down at the green dress stretched flat over her thighs. "I've never mentioned this before," she said slowly, "but I've thought about it quite a bit, and I've heard the hands talking about it. You look almost enough like Frank Graben to be his brother. I've even thought a time or two you were him, when I saw you a piece off."

He sighed and looked ill at ease. "I've been wondering when someone would bring that up."

She met his glance. "Then you noticed the resemblance yourself?"

He slowly nodded. "He was about the same height and build and his hair was about the same color as mine. But the main thing was that we were both wearing black hats and dark clothes. I think that was what everyone noticed."

"Have you got any brothers?" she asked.

He again shook his head. "I was the only child. My father left before I was born and never came back. It was during the border wars between Kansas and Missouri in the late forties and early fifties. He came over with some Missouri raiders and was wounded pretty bad. My mother found him lying unconscious in the pasture below her father's house and nursed him back to health and married him. But he disappeared soon after that when some men came looking for him and she never saw him again. She always believed he went back to Missouri and married a local girl he'd grown up with and just didn't mention having a wife in Kansas. My grandfather went looking for him and found the small town he claimed to be from, but there wasn't anyone around there named Knell. So he either lied about his name or where he was from. But I don't want to bore you with the story of my life. I've never told anyone that before. But I've got a feeling you've been wondering about who I am and where I came from, so I thought I'd tell you."

Kate Barlow's eyes were bright with interest. "From what you've just said, you could be that man's brother, or half brother, without even knowing about it!"

Knell came close to smiling—about as close as he ever came. "That would be quite a coincidence, wouldn't it?"

"Hasn't the same thought occurred to you? That he might be your half brother?"

He thought for a moment, then slowly shook his head. "I'd say the chances are pretty slight. I never said anything about it to my mother, but from what she told me I always figured those men who were looking for my father caught up with him and killed him, or he would have come back or at least sent for her. You probably wouldn't think it to look at me, but my mother was considered the most beautiful girl in that part of Kansas. I can still remember when men were sighing over her and talking about 'that black-eyed beauty,' as they called her. I think every man around there was broken-hearted when she died. And I have a feeling that one of the reasons they didn't like my father was that she married him instead of one of them. Then when they found out he'd been one of the Missouri raiders who'd caused so much trouble around there, that was sort of the last straw. But if they did find him and killed him, they never admitted it, because they knew she'd never forgive them if she ever found out about it."

"Maybe your father already had a family when he married your mother," Kate said. "Frank Graben looks several years older than you."

"That's what I thought when I first saw him," Knell agreed. "But after I got a closer look at him, I decided he was probably two or three years younger than me. I'd say he's not much over twenty-seven or twenty-eight, and I'll soon be thirty-one."

He stopped suddenly as if he had said something he had not intended to, and Kate Barlow did not miss the half-startled look on his lean dark face.

She smiled faintly. "You helped him get away, didn't you? I've had a feeling all along that was what you were doing those two days you were gone, instead of looking for him like you claimed. I figured you did it because you were his brother, and I've been keeping an eye on you. I didn't fire you because I thought that as long as you were here, he might come back, and then we'd have another chance at him. Now after what you've told me—I believe most of what you said, but I still have the feeling you helped him get away because you thought he might be your half brother."

Knell shook his head, and his dark eyes were hard. "I helped him get away because I didn't think he killed your father, and because he'd got nothing but a raw deal from everyone since he set foot in this country. I can understand how you feel about him, because of what you've been told and what you believe. But I can also understand how he feels, and I hope to God he doesn't come back, because if he does, what happened before wasn't even a sample."

"I'm afraid you're hoping in vain," Kate Barlow said, "because he's back. I saw him when I went to town."

Knell let out a long sigh. Or perhaps it was only the wind haunting the frame house in that bleak empty desert. "What do you aim to do?" he asked.

She remained silent for a time, looking down at her folded hands in her lap. She was barely twenty but at that moment she looked closer to thirty. Losing her father and the man she thought she loved had aged her beyond her years. Finally she stirred and said in a tired still voice, "This isn't an easy decision for me. I've always hated to admit I was wrong about anything. But this time I'm afraid we were all wrong about Frank Graben. Except you. I wish you'd spoken up a lot sooner. It might have saved a lot of trouble."

"I thought about it," he said. "But I'm in the habit of minding my own business and keeping my mouth shut. It's the only way to stay out of trouble. And at the time I didn't figure anyone was in the mood to listen. I figured if I said anything I'd find myself about as welcome around here as Graben was."

"You were probably right, too," she admitted.

He nodded. "It might have been just as well," he said. "If you plan to send us after him again, I guess I might as well ask for my time now. Ganging up on one man is not my idea of a fair fight."

She shook her head. "I'm going to give orders for him to be let alone. It's going to be hard for me to get used to the idea of him walking around free, after feeling the way I have about him for so long. But you and Aunt Jill wouldn't have both told me so much the same story if it wasn't true, and I don't see how he could have done anything but what he did do. It's what almost any man with any pride would have done, or tried to do."

"I'm glad you see it that way," Knell said with obvious relief. Then a look of worry touched his dark eyes. "Ma'am, I don't know quite how to say this, but I think I know what will happen when you tell the men to let him alone. They will make out like they're going to do as you wish, but when they're out of your sight it will be Graf Stoker's orders they follow, and he'll make up some story to tell you, like he did before."

Her green eyes turned cold with anger. "Go tell him to come in here," she said.

Knell silently nodded and left the room. A few minutes later the tall, rugged, black-bearded foreman came in with his hat in his hand, but scowling darkly, as if he knew something was wrong.

Kate Barlow regarded him with her cool green eyes. "Did Knell tell you?" she asked.

"He said you wanted to see me. He didn't tell me nothin' else."

She nodded as if satisfied, and said after a moment, "I was in town today. Guess who I saw."

"Who?"

"Frank Graben."

She was watching him closely as she said the name, and she saw him rough-hewn face register the shock of surprise. It was almost as if he had received a blow. But like a fighter who loved combat, he quickly recovered from the blow and a look of excitement, of gloating anticipation, came into his eyes. His heavy voice rose in a bellow of amazement and outrage. "You mean that son of a bitch had the gall to come back here?"

She nodded. "It looks that way."

Stoker could barely contain his excitement. "Why didn't you tell me sooner? I'll get the boys and ride into town after the bastard."

He put on his hat and headed for the door, but she stopped him, saying sharply, "Just a minute! I'll tell you when to ride into town after someone."

He turned and stared at her in wonder, his bearded mouth hanging open.

"I'd like for you to tell me again just what happened in town the night Carl and Shorty were killed," she said in a cold, taunting voice.

He studied her face carefully, and then the familiar scowl darkened his brow. "What did Knell tell you?" he asked.

"Why did you lie about what happened?" she asked. "You must have known we'd find out the truth sooner or later. You probably got Pa killed, did you know that? If he'd known the truth, he never would have gone after Frank Graben and he wouldn't have been shot."

Graf Stoker snorted. "He would of gone after him no matter how I said it happened, I just told him what I knowed he'd want to hear, that's all. Whitey Barlow never cared about the truth. It if wasn't what he wanted to hear, then he didn't want to hear it—it was that simple. And it sure never tuck me long to find that out. If I wanted to keep him smilin' and happy, I always just told him what he wanted to hear, and everything went fine."

"Until it got him killed," she said, her eyes icy with bitterness. "Well, I'm running this ranch now, and from now on you better start telling me the truth, not what you think I want to hear. If I find out you've been lying to me again, I'll get someone I can trust. Is that understood?"

The big foreman stood scowling silently and murderously at a spot on the floor, his jaws clenching and unclenching as if he were chewing on something he could not quite swallow.

Kate Barlow's voice rose angrily as she repeated, "Is that understood?"

He swallowed his anger and his arrogance with difficulty and managed to say hoarsely, "It's understood. But I think you're makin' a bad mistake. Runnin' a ranch this size ain't no job for a woman like you to dirty her hands with. Things has to be done time to time you'd be a lot happier not ever knowin' about. When Whitey was killed I just figgered you'd let me go on runnin' the ranch like I know he'd want me to run it, and I think in time you'll realize that's the best thing to do."

"You may be right," she said. "But until then we'll try it my way."

The foreman heaved a great sigh and there was a look of doom in his eyes. "What about Graben?" he asked.

"I want all of you to leave him alone," she said. "I just hope he leaves us alone, after what we've done to him."

"What we've done to him!" Stoker echoed. "What about what he done to Carl and Shorty?"

"Are you back on that again?" she cried. "What choice did they give him? But it was just as much your fault as theirs. Instead of egging them on you should have stopped them and kept them out of trouble. If anything like that ever happens again, I won't just fire you, I'll run you out of the country!"

"All right," he grunted, and stalked out.

He went directly to the bunkhouse and found Knell sitting on his bunk, cleaning his gun. Scowling, the foreman asked, "Knell, what in hell did you tell her?"

Knell glanced up at the foreman's angry, bearded face. His own face remained calm and there was not the slightest trace of fear in his dark gray eyes. "I told her the truth," he said. "I figured it was time someone did."

"What the hell you tryin' to do?" Stoker roared. "Don't you know nothin'? You don't tell a woman the truth! You tell them what they want to hear!"

Some of the hands laughed, but the others stared at Knell with hard eyes. They had never really trusted him, and they had always resented his silent aloofness. But now they resented him even more for shooting off his mouth to the boss lady. They saw it as backstabbing betrayal and a scurvy attempt to worm his way into her affections at their expense.

"You try pullin' something like that again," Stoker warned him darkly, "and there's ways of shuttin' you up for keeps."

"I'll keep it in mind," Knell said quietly and went on cleaning his gun.

"You do that."

After a lonely supper in the hotel dining room, Graben sat in the lobby and smoked a cigar. He was aware from time to time that Sam Dauber opened the door of the small room behind the desk and peered out at him. Graben did not look around, but kept his attention on the street through the open door. The afternoon had been hot, but a cool dry breeze drifted in off the desert, and in his mind he could see the dark brush out beyond the town stirring and rustling in the breeze and the darker mountains rimming the desert in the distance. It would be nice, he thought, just to get his horse and ride out and keep riding. That was what he wanted to do, and what he would have done five months ago if everyone had not tried so hard to make him leave. But they had tried to run him out, and then they had tried to kill him, and that was why he had come back. He had his pride. And now he had a score to settle. Now they would have to finish the job.

The general store across the street was dark, as dark as the old abandoned shack next to it. The barbershop was also dark. He wondered how many people in this town were crouched in their houses, watching the street, waiting for him to leave the hotel. Waiting to see if he would be shot down as he stepped outside.

He did not envy those people. Most of them would probably still be alive long after he was dead, but he did not envy them. They could not understand a man like him and to them his life no doubt seemed bleak and empty and without meaning or purpose, but he preferred it to theirs, however short it might be. He preferred his own somber, solitary thoughts to their silly chatter and malicious gossip. He would rather be sitting here waiting for a bullet than to be crouching behind a dark window waiting to see if a bolder, braver man walked out in the street and was shot down. It was better to die with courage and dignity than to live forever as a trembling coward filled with self-hatred.

The door behind the desk opened again and this time Dauber approached unsteadily and stood looking down at him with a kind of bitter resentment in his bleary eyes. His face was flushed and contorted almost beyond recognition, his hair and his clothes were disheveled and he bore only a slight resemblance to the neat, almost dapper man he was when sober. He made a vague, uncertain gesture as if he had trouble remembering what he meant to say, and then it came back to him and his eyes cleared a little. "I wouldn't sit there if I was you," he said.

"Why not?" Graben asked dryly.

"Just take my word for it," Dauber said, glancing through the door and out across the dark street. "That's about the worst place you could be. And if I was you I'd keep away from the windows too." Then he went unsteadily back across the carpeted floor and into the small room behind the desk, closing the door behind him.

Graben sat lost in thought and slowly smoked his cigar, a look of puzzled gravity on his weather-beaten dark face. Dauber was about the last person he had expected to warn him of danger. Then he remembered that Max Rumford, who evidently had no love for him, had once let him use the back door of his saloon to avoid the risk of being shot down if he left by the front. And a little light of comprehension suddenly flashed inside his head and a grim smile twisted his lips. Both Rumford and Dauber seemed to know that he was going to be killed, and neither minded that, but neither wanted it to happen in his establishment, for then there would be questions to answer if the county sheriff ever rode over this way to look into the matter.

Graben was oddly elated at this thought. A kind of bitter reckless joy surged through him like silent laughter, and he wanted to rush out into a cold wind or a storm had there only been one handy. He wanted no favors from anyone at this late day and certainly not from his enemies, and it was a relief to know that they were thinking of their own welfare instead of his. He did not blame them. It no longer mattered what they did. He was so far down the dark lonely

trail of his own bitter isolation that he could think of his enemies
with detached amusement. All their scheming and planning, all their
hopes and fears and hates and petty jealousies—in the end it would
all come to nothing, for their fate was already sealed, just as his own
was sealed.

CHAPTER 12

Frank Graben rose and went up to his room, but he did not light the lamp. In the dark he found his saddlebags and blanket roll and moved them into the corner by the door. Then he stood at the window and watched the dark deserted street, as he knew most of the town was doing. They were watching for him, but he was watching for someone else.

And finally the short stocky shape he was watching for appeared, trudging rather rapidly along the street with his bare head turned to peer up at Graben's dark window as he passed. Barney Ludlow had a curious, awkward way of walking, with his knees wide apart and his toes turned outward as if his feet were trying to go in opposite directions. Graben could recognize that walk by the sound alone—and in the utter silence of the town the footsteps made a loud racket on the hard-packed street. Had any doubt remained, it was erased when the man pushed his way into the restaurant. Ludlow apparently had no wife and took all his meals in the restaurant, staying as long as an hour to talk to the elderly woman who ran the place, and had tried to run Graben out of it. Failing at that, she had gone into the kitchen and remained there until he left.

Graben had got his horse and left town before when Ludlow was in the restaurant, and he planned to do so again. That way it might be a while before anyone found out he was gone. The longer the better. He enjoyed the thought of them waiting on edge to see what he would do. And in fact that was why he was leaving, to keep them in suspense a while longer. For even after they found out he was gone, they would know this time that he would be back, and they would be scheming and plotting ways to get rid of him—permanently—before he could cause any more trouble.

He watched the restaurant a few minutes to make sure Ludlow did not just duck in and out again this time to fool him. Once satisfied this was not the case, he wasted no more time. Crossing the dark room to the door, he bent to pick up the saddlebags and blanket roll, then let himself out and went silently along the dimly lit hall to the rear stairs. A minute later he carefully opened the back door and stepped outside.

Even before he realized what it was, something warned him instantly of danger and he stepped quickly aside, drawing the double-action Colt from his waistband. Then at the edge of the brush he saw what it was that had warned him—glass gleaming in the dark, and too high up to be on the ground. A moment later a bullet splintered the door behind him and he fired back at the muzzle flash. He squeezed the trigger twice and heard the man cry out and saw him topple forward out of the brush and fall on his face, dropping the rifle.

Graben went forward with the gun in his hand and toed the man over onto his back. He did not bend down or strike a match. It wasn't necessary. Even in the dark he knew that the small man in the business suit was Hiram Goodman, the storekeeper. Apparently Goodman had not liked being blackmailed, but Graben would never have guessed the man had it in him to try something like this. He had only pulled that stunt on the storekeeper in a moment of inspired vindictiveness, to get even with him for not wanting to do business with him, and had intended all along to return the money—once he satisfied himself that Goodman was not one of those plotting to kill him. But now there did not seem to be any point in returning the money to a dead man.

A cool wind rattled the brush. The back door of the hotel opened and he cut a sharp glance that way, then relaxed when he saw the slender outline of Jill Dauber. She stood there silently for a moment peering out into the darkness. Then she said softly, "Frank?"

It sounded odd to hear her use his first name in a worried, inquisitive tone, and he was silent for several seconds thinking about it before he replied. "Over here."

"Are you all right?" she asked in the same low, worried tone, as if afraid someone would hear her.

"I am. But he ain't."

"Who is it?"

"Goodman."

He walked back toward her and she noticed the saddlebags and blanket roll, the gun which he now returned to his waistband. "Are you leaving?" she asked.

"For now," he said. "But I'll be back." Then he gestured toward the dead man and asked, "Any idea why he'd try to kill me?"

She looked that way and her voice sounded hoarse when she spoke. "I think I know why he did it. But I'd rather not say now."

Graben studied her curiously for a moment, but the dim light was behind her and he could tell nothing about her face in the dark. He shifted the saddlebags and blanket roll on his left shoulder and said, "Well, I better go before anyone gets up the nerve to take a look back here. I left the key and some money on the bureau."

She closed the door softly behind her and came a little closer, looking up at his face. "When do you think you'll be back?" she asked.

He shrugged, glancing off across the desert toward the mountains in the distance. "Hard to say." Then his lips twisted in a small cold smile. "I want a few people in this town to sweat a while trying to figger out what I'm going to do and when I'm going to do it. That storekeeper may have been one of them, but I think he tried to get me for another reason."

"Maybe for more reasons than you think," Jill Dauber murmured. "I've about decided to tell you something. But now I'll have to wait until you come back."

She did not need to tell him that Dauber was probably inside listening, and might even be watching through the window. Graben merely nodded, touched his hat and headed for the livery stable in long strides. Barney Ludlow did not appear. Graben saddled the blue roan and headed west across the desert, wondering about Jill Dauber's last cryptic remark. Tell him what?

He tried not to think about Hiram Goodman. In his time he had often seen the unhappy results of what he thought of as boyish pranks, and had never played games until people started playing games with him. Now, his little blackmailing prank had resulted in the death of a man who was perhaps innocent of any crime other than the understandable desire to get even with him. It was true that Graben had once seen, in an old newspaper, a picture that bore a slight resem-

blance to Goodman, and he remembered reading that the owner of
the face, one Peabody, had been somehow mixed up in the theft of a
great deal of money from the bank where he worked. But the details
were hazy in Graben's mind and in truth he doubted if Goodman
had been Peabody. He had only used that story to frighten the little
man. Whether true or not, it could ruin his reputation in a place like
Hackamore. But Graben had never seriously intended to spread that
story, any more than he had planned to keep the money.

Now Goodman was dead and that was something he would have
to think about sometime. But he did not want to think about it now.
He had vowed that nothing would keep him from doing what he had
set out to do, and now he renewed that vow.

A few miles from town the trail dipped into a brush-choked hollow where the breeze felt a lot cooler, and he paused long enough to
put on the short black corduroy jacket. This was a good time of the
year for night riding. In a few more weeks it would be too hot even at
night and the flies and mosquitoes would be unbearable. Graben did
not care for summer. But then he was not crazy about winter either.
Spring and fall were his seasons, and he found himself thinking it
would be nice if he could live to see a good many more of each. For a
moment he almost weakened in his resolve to stay in this troubled
range and die if need be—but only for a moment. Then his face hardened and he rode on toward the foothills.

It was near midnight when he reached the Wilkins place. He had
decided that if the shack was dark he would ride on by. But a feeble
yellow light leaked through the small window and the unchinked
logs, and he walked his horse down the rocky slope toward the shack.
Wilkins heard the ring of the shod hoofs on the rocks and opened the
door, watching him halt in the shadows twenty feet away and ease
his weight in the saddle.

"Light and rest," the squatter said in a worried tone, studying the
face in the dark shadow of the hat brim.

Graben stepped down slowly and went toward the door, leaving
the reins hanging. When he entered the light Wilkins again peered
at his hard face and cold gray eyes.

"I had a feelin' that would be you," the squatter said. "I saw you
in town. Ain't been back long myself."

Graben silently stepped inside after him and closed the door
and stood with his back to it, his glance taking in the room. There
were two beds. The stout Mrs. Wilkins sat on one darning socks. Her

daughter sat on the other reading a book. The girl gave Graben a quick scared look and then dropped her glance, a spot of color appearing in her pale cheeks. Wilkins got a chair for Graben and then sat down on the bed beside his wife.

Graben turned the chair around, straddled it and scowled at the squatter. "Cushing and his men been around lately?"

"The wife said Lum Mulock stopped here for supper," Wilkins said, nervously running his fingers through his thinning hair. "We ain't seen the others in about a week."

After a moment Graben asked, "Remember that day I came here with them?"

Wilkins nodded. "I was just thinkin' about that a minute ago."

"What did Cushing tell you about me when he came in?" Graben asked.

Wilkins looked uneasily at his wife before answering. "Why, nothing, as I recall. Barely mentioned your name."

Graben noticed that Mrs. Wilkins gave her husband a quick, hard look. But then she went on with her sewing and didn't say anything.

"Did Whitey Barlow and his men come by here after we left?" Graben asked.

Wilkins rubbed his chin, saying, "No, I don't believe I remember seein' them."

Without missing a stitch in her sewing, Mrs. Wilkins said, "You know very well they come by here, Homer Wilkins."

Wilkins gave her a startled look, then shifted his glance to Graben and showed eroded teeth in a miserable laugh. "That's right, I believe they did come by here. Imagine her rememberin' after all this time."

"What did you tell them?" Graben asked.

Wilkins again looked startled. "What do you mean?"

"You know damn well what I mean," Graben told him flatly.

"Why, I don't recollect tellin' them anything."

"Liar," Mrs. Wilkins said. "If you ain't got the guts to stand up to a man, then don't be sayin' things behind his back."

Wilkins got red in the face. "Now, woman, you ain't got no call to talk to me that way," he said hoarsely. "What are you tryin' to do to me anyway?"

"I guess I know all I need to know," Graben said. He glanced at Molly Wilkins, who was watching him with wide, frightened eyes, but quickly lowered her glance when he looked at her. He grunted in irritation, "Wilkins, tell your daughter she can relax. I've had my mind on killing certain men so much lately that I've sort of lost interest in pretty girls. Cushing's men are the ones she better watch out for, if they ever get her alone. I wouldn't harm a hair on her silly head. Yet I'm the one she's afraid of."

"You've got sort of a mean look," Wilkins said with another sickly laugh. "And Molly knows about you killin' them folks in town. She can't stand the thought of blood."

"Then you shouldn't be butchering any stray beefs around her," Graben said. He meant it as a jibe about the squatter's connection with Cushing's men, who sometimes left a Barlow steer or maverick for him to eat on. But the taunt was lost on Wilkins.

"Molly won't hardly eat a bite of meat," he said. "Pore girl pecks at her food like a sick bird. I guess that's how she keeps her slender figger. Her Ma was like that 'fore she started puttin' on weight."

Mrs. Wilkins' dark eyes hardened and her fat cheeks wobbled in anger. "You shouldn't be talkin' that way to strangers, Homer Wilkins," she snarled.

Wilkins gave her a baffled look, his mouth hanging open. "There just ain't no way to please you, is there, woman? When I lie to him, you get mad about that. And when I tell him the truth, you get mad about that!"

"Well, there's things a body shouldn't oughter talk about one way or the other," Mrs. Wilkins said, looking for holes she might have missed in the sock. "Lord knows the girl is too purty for her own good, without you bringin' it to everybody's attention. It's like you're shovin' her at ever' man that rides by, when the good Lord knows I'm a better judge of suitable prospects."

"Well, I don't know about that," Wilkins said, "from the way you talk. How many's the time have you said if you had any brains you never would of married me?"

"Well, I reckon a woman can learn from her mistakes, can't she? They do say experience is the best teacher."

They seemed to have forgotten Graben, and he stared at them in amazement. If this was what marriage was like, he wanted no part of it. And it amused him that his presence here had excited this stout woman's protective instincts toward her daughter. She had already rejected him as a possible suitor for the girl before the thought of becoming one occurred to him. He rose with a harsh laugh and left the shack, thinking that he had not missed anything. Not a thing. Yet there was a lost, sick, lonely feeling in him as he mounted and rode away into the dark windy night.

It had been a mistake to stop at the squatter shack. He had a strong hunch that Rube Cushing had left some message for Wilkins to pass on to Whitey Barlow the day Barlow was killed and Graben himself seriously wounded. But at the last moment he had decided not to force Wilkins to talk, although it would have probably been easy. It had even seemed that Mrs. Wilkins might divulge the information without much persuading, not realizing what the result might be. But what could Graben have done even if he had obtained proof of the squatter's complicity? Killed him or beaten him up in front of his wife and daughter? What good would that have done? And Graben hated to think of the look of horror on Molly Wilkins's face if she had witnessed such a thing.

Graben rode on toward the shadowy foothills, his weather-beaten face bleak and still. After a time he became aware that the night chill had penetrated his thin jacket, but he did not change it for the warmer corduroy coat. He almost welcomed the cold. Anything to take his mind off his oppressive thoughts.

The country became rougher as he neared the foothills. He avoided the well-defined trail that led to the rustler shack, but paralleled the trail at a distance. A pale blade of a moon hung above the rising dark mountains, shedding only a little light and no heat. The stars were even colder and more remote. Like a few men he had admired but never much liked. Men a good deal like himself. He entered a narrow valley between two rocky slopes and followed it until it became a mere gully dodging around rocks and stunted cedars trembling in the cold wind. Climbing out, he soon entered a scrub forest of pinon and juniper and circled through it until he was on a rough steep slope above the rustler shack. Here he halted among some rocks and for a time he sat his saddle looking down on the dark shack with cold eyes, while inside him the gray coals of an old anger began to smolder and burn.

Dismounting, he wrapped the reins around a knotty limb, checked the birdshead Colt and unhurriedly made his way down through the rocks and trees on foot. When he was fifty yards from the shack he halted again, the gun in his hand. But now he was more interested in the pole corral than the shack. There was only one horse in the corral, and that puzzled him. Of course, it was not unusual for ranchers to turn all their horses out at night to graze. But Cushing and his men were not ranchers, they were rustlers, and rustlers liked to keep some fast horses handy in case they were needed in a hurry. So Graben concluded that they were probably all gone except for one man left behind to guard the shack—and watch for Graben. But where would that man be? It depended on who the man was and what he was supposed to do if Graben showed up.

Graben remained where he was for nearly a half hour, watching and listening, hoping to see or hear something that would tell him where the man was. But he saw no movement, heard no sound except for the normal night sounds and the dark trees rustling their branches in the wind. And finally, using the wind to cover any slight noise he made, he eased on down toward the shack.

At last, standing outside the small log house, he heard someone inside snoring loudly. A faint smile twisted his lips as he moved soundlessly along the wall to the window and peered in. Even in the dark he could see the sleeping man sitting at the table with his head pillowed on his folded arms.

Moving like a shadow, Graben went around to the door, pushed it open and stepped inside, his eyes on the man seated at the table. The man did not move as Graben circled around behind him and prodded him with the muzzle of the gun.

"Come alive."

The man grunted and his head shot up in surprise. "Huh? Is it time to get up?"

"Stay where you are. Where are the others?"

The man in the chair stiffened, suddenly realizing that something was wrong. He was silent a moment and then he asked in a scared voice, "Who're you?"

"Just a ghost. I'm the man you bastards killed."

A tremor went through the one in the chair. It was the big towhaired boy who called himself Billy the Kid, although at the moment his unsteady voice sounded more like that of a frightened girl. "Graben?"

"You guessed it. Now let me repeat my original question. Where are the others?"

"They went to town. I—I think they was lookin' for you."

"Wish I'd known they were coming. It would have saved me a trip."

"You didn't meet them?"

"I avoided the trail. I didn't want to get what Whitey Barlow got. Or what I got after I left here."

"That wasn't me done that," the Kid said nervously.

"Then I guess it had to be Lutter," Graben said. "Cushing and Mulock were here and France was with Barlow's men."

"Pete said it wasn't him neither," the Kid said. "But he can explain it better than I can."

"I'm sure he can. Cushing told him exactly what to say."

The Kid sat stiff and silent. Graben shifted the birdshead Colt to his left hand and with his right reached for the holstered revolver at the Kid's hip. When his hand closed on the familiar stock of the gun, he grunted in surprise. "You wouldn't be wearing my Russian pistols, would you, Kid?"

The Kid's voice trembled with fear. "I bought them from Lutter, 'cause I lost my gun."

"Lost it?" Graben said in a tone of amazement.

The Kid moved slightly in the chair, a kind of shrug. "I don't know what happened to it. One day it wasn't in my holster, and I ain't seen it since. So Lutter sold me the ones you had. I never thought about you comin' back and—"

"I'll bet you didn't," Graben grunted. "Unbuckle the belt and lean forward." The Kid did as he was told. Graben grasped the shell belt at the small of the Kid's back and lifted the belt and holstered guns and strapped them around his own lean waist, keeping the birdshead Colt in his left hand. He pulled back a chair and sat down beside the Kid, watching him with cold eyes. "Lutter say how he got them?"

"He said, but I might get it mixed up if I tried to tell you," the Kid said nervously. "It would be better if he told you hisself when they get back."

"I'll be here," Graben said grimly. "You might as well relax, Kid. It may be a long wait."

CHAPTER 13

Sitting at the rough plank table in the dark shack, Graben heard the wind in the pinons and junipers. In his mind he looked down the long slope toward the windswept plain. He saw the wind blowing dust and making its lonesome music around the Wilkins shack. He saw Molly Wilkins's pale face and frightened dark eyes, and he felt an odd futility settling inside him. He had not wanted to frighten her, yet it was obvious that she had been a lot more frightened than her father, who had seemed unaware that he was in any real danger, fearing at worst that he might be exposed as a talebearer.

Graben sighed and rubbed a hand across his face, feeling the dust and grit that had settled there during his ride across the windy plain. He reflected that it was usually that way—he always seemed to frighten the people he meant no harm, and as a result they felt more at ease around his enemies and took their side, more often than not. For that, he knew he should have blamed himself for his impatience with people and his inability to get along with them, but as a rule he was more inclined to blame them for their stupidity, their weaknesses and their poor judgment.

His mouth twisted in disgust, more at himself than anyone else. He was sick of his life and tired of being at odds with the whole world. At the same time he felt the hopeless anger and disgust in him propelling him irrevocably toward his doom. He felt himself on the edge of losing all control and restraint and becoming like a few hate-crazed killers he had known, men who would shoot you for looking at them the wrong way. If Graben lasted much longer he would reach that point himself.

That was one reason why he had come back. It was not in him to die without a fight, so it was better to die fighting men who deserved the worst that could happen to them. And if he was killed himself, which seemed likely, well, that was the only way for a man like him to go, with a gun in his hand, trying to take as many of his enemies with him as possible.

He turned his cold eyes toward the Kid in the dark, resenting him for sitting there like a lump and not putting up any kind of fight. But he was even more annoyed because he could feel no real anger at the gawky youth and had trouble thinking of him as an enemy, despite the fact that he was one of the Cushing gang and had perhaps even played some small part in their attempt to kill him.

"Billy the Kid," Graben sneered. "Why didn't you tell them you were Wild Bill Hickok? You're more his size, and he's been dead for so long they've probably forgot about it, if they ever even heard."

The Kid sat silent, as if debating with himself whether to admit that he had lied about his name. But Graben was in no mood to listen to any confessions. He got up and restlessly paced the floor, pausing to peer out the window. The sky in the east was turning gray. The wind had died. The pinons and junipers stood dark and motionless, waiting in the pre-dawn hush for the morning breeze to bring them back to life.

"What time you figger they'll be back?" he asked.

The Kid raised his head. His voice sounded relieved that Graben had changed the subject. "I figgered they'd ride in here about daylight," he said. "Hungry as bears and yellin' for some breakfast."

"You don't want to disappoint them, then," Graben said. "Go ahead and rustle up some grub. By the way, where's your rifle?"

"I let Lum Mulock borrow it," the Kid said as he rose. "He never found the one he loaned you that day."

"The one he killed Whitey Barlow with?" Graben asked. "That must have been Cushing's idea for him to plant that gun on me. Mulock ain't smart enough to think of something like that all by himself."

"I don't know about that," the Kid said uneasily, kneeling at the fireplace to kindle a fire. "All I know is what they told me."

Graben sat down at the end of the table and checked the Smith

& Wesson .44 Russians in the dim gray light creeping into the room. "I can't figger out whether they lied to you, or you're lying to me," he said. "I can understand why you'd lie to me easy enough, but I don't know why they'd keep it a secret from you for so long. Maybe they didn't trust you to keep your mouth shut."

"That could be it," the Kid admitted, clearing his throat. "They don't seem to think I'm too smart in some ways."

"I wonder what ever gave them that idea."

"I don't know," the Kid said. He grew motionless, his head cocked in a listening attitude. Then he reached casually for the coffeepot. "I'll have to get some water from the spring if you want coffee."

"You set tight," Graben told him, rising and moving to the window. "I heard them too." He gave the Kid a sharp glance over his shoulder. "You've got good ears, and maybe you ain't quite as dumb as you let on. You were going to sneak down there and warn them— just when I was beginning to think we could be friends."

The Kid looked at him uncertainly. "What made you think we could be friends?" he asked, as if genuinely puzzled.

"I don't know," Graben admitted. "You just never seemed much like one of them. But I guess I was wrong." He made an impatient gesture, scowling. "Go on with your cooking. The coffee water will have to wait."

"There's a little in here. More'n I thought."

"I figgered there was."

With a grunt he turned back to the window, looking down toward the trail where it rose into view at the corner of the pole corral. Now he could clearly hear the horses coming up the trail, though he could not yet see them or their riders.

He tucked the birdshead Colt into his waistband and drew one of the Russians, giving the Kid another cold glance over his shoulder. "Did you take good care of my guns?"

"Best I could." After a moment the boy added as he sliced bacon into the frying pan, "I ain't shot them much. Didn't have no shells to waste. Pickin's has been sort of slim around here. We been tryin' not to rile the Star hands by stealin' too many cows. Cushing don't want no trouble with them. He says there's too many of them and not enough of us."

"Mulock let on like you boys and the Star hands were plumb cozy," Graben grunted, again watching out the window.

"That's only 'cause we've gone out of our way not to get them mad, like I said. But I think Rube and the others is gettin' tired of starvin' to please them."

"Be quiet," Graben said. He stood to one side of the window with his head cocked, listening. He could no longer hear the horses. They had stopped on the shoulder of the slope just out of sight.

Then Cushing's voice called, "Graben! You in there?" He sounded a little nervous.

"I'm here!" he called back.

"We're comin' on up!" Cushing yelled. "I want to talk to you! I give you my word we won't try nothin'!"

"Come ahead!" Graben replied. Then he added a deliberate taunt, "And try anything you think you can get away with!"

He heard the fat man laugh. But then Cushing said in a hurt tone, "You got us all wrong, Graben! We're your friends!" A moment later he walked his horse into view, holding his open right hand up at shoulder level, the others close behind him. There was a worried grin on his bloated round face as he peered at the shack. "Don't shoot now," he said.

"You've got *me* all wrong," Graben said in a dry, mocking voice, watching them through a crack in the unchinked log wall. "I'm your friend, too."

The big man smiled, pretending not to notice the irony. He heaved himself out of the saddle and waddled toward the shack, leaving the horse for his men to care for. Graben kept one eye on them and saw them watching the shack as they began unsaddling. Cushing pushed the door open and came in with his jolly fake smile. He gave the Kid a mild indifferent glance and then turned his full attention on Graben. He seemed not to notice the gun in Graben's hand.

"I'm mighty glad to see you back, son," he said.

A small cold smile twisted Graben's lips. "I'll bet you are." The gun remained in his hand, though he did not bother to point it at the fat man.

Cushing gave him a closer look, but the happy round face did not change. What he saw on Graben's lean tough face he had expected to see. He went to the fireplace and held his open hands toward the blaze, sniffing the aromas of frying bacon and boiling coffee, but he seemed not to notice the cook. "My, that smells good." He turned back around to look at Graben, still smiling the meaningless smile of a man who could kill you and keep smiling. "From what they said about that blood on the ground, I figgered you prob'ly crawled off someplace and died."

"Sorry to disappoint you," Graben said, also smiling, though it was a much colder and bleaker smile. "Seems like a lot of people around here had that idea."

"How did you manage to get away without leavin' no sign them Star hands could follow?" Cushing asked curiously. "I mean, you bein' wounded and all. Looks like they could of found some blood or tracks or somethin' to trail you by, but there wasn't nothin'. Not a trace."

Graben shrugged. "Maybe they just weren't as good as they thought they were."

"That could be," Cushing admitted. He grinned. "Come to think about it, they prob'ly ain't all that good. If they was, they would of caught us stealin' their cows before now. But that Knell feller worries me. I got a feelin he could catch us at it if he really wanted to. He's the one they found standin' by that spot of blood, did you know that? But here comes Pete and the others. Let him tell you what he told me." He turned toward the door as Lutter, Mulock and France came in. "Pete, tell Graben what you think happened the day he was shot."

The dark lanky rider looked at Graben and scowled. "Well, I was on that high peak watchin' for Barlow's men when I heard a shot. It came from down in that narrow valley and I decided to take a look. I found you layin' there and I thought you was dead. I figgered it must have been one of the Star hands who shot you and I didn't know how many of them was around there. But I didn't want to leave your guns for them bastards, so I bent down to get them, and just then somebody started shootin' at me and I got the hell away from there. I didn't get a look at him, but it must have been that Knell, and I guess he was the one who shot you. There wasn't anyone else around there."

"Just you and him?" Graben asked.

Lutter scowled and nodded.

"What about my wallet?"

Lutter shook his head. "I don't know nothin' about it. All I had time for was the guns." Then he said, "I guess the Kid told you I sold them to him when he lost his?"

"He told me."

A look of defiance came into Lutter's narrow face. "I kept them for you for quite a while, but finally I decided you was dead. I thought you was dead when I saw you layin' there, or I never would of taken them in the first place. Then they said they couldn't find you, alive or dead, so I didn't know what to think."

Graben was aware that they were all watching him to see if he was swallowing Lutter's story. He glanced at Lum Mulock and saw the stupid grin on the chunky man's hard found face. He kept his attention on Mulock as he said, "Who killed Whitey Barlow?"

Mulock's eyes shifted away and his swarthy face reddened a little in a look of discomfort. But the stupid grin remained. The man with the twisted face stood beside him, also grinning. He never took his amused and malicious eyes off Graben.

Rube Cushing stirred and spoke. "We figger it was one of Whitey's own men who killed him. He could be a hard man to work for at time, from what they say, and they prob'ly figgered if he was out of the way they could do as they pleased." He smiled. "And I guess they liked the idea of workin' for his daughter. So they killed him and tried to blame it on you."

Graben stared at the fat man in amazement, almost choking on the lie Cushing seemed so confident he would swallow. For a moment a bitter anger scalded his insides and he had trouble breathing. Cushing had planned to eliminate Whitey Barlow and Graben on the same day, letting Graben take the blame for Barlow's death and Cushing and his men get the credit for getting Barlow's alleged murderer. That had not worked out quite according to plan, and now he was trying to blame the Star hands for everything that had happened, while making the rustlers seem like innocent bystanders. And they were all watching Graben and smiling, confident that he would swallow every word of it. They were beginning almost to believe it themselves, it sounded so convincing.

And Graben might have swallowed it, except for a few minor little details. He knew almost beyond a doubt that Lum Mulock had killed Whitey Barlow. And he knew almost beyond a doubt that Knell, the man they claimed had shot him, Graben, was the one who had in fact carried him away to safety, when everyone else was trying to find him and kill him.

The burning anger slowly subsided, he slowly relaxed, and said almost casually, "That feller Knell—what did you say he looked like?"

"A lot like you in some ways," Cushing said, watching him with a trace of uneasiness. "About the same height and build. Hair a lot like yours. Gray eyes, but a lot darker than yours. Usually wears dark clothes and a black hat. You'll know him when you see him."

Graben silently nodded. The description matched that given him by the grizzled prospector. The old prospector had thought that the man who had brought him might be his brother. It gave Graben an odd feeling. Except for the eyes, he might have believed Knell—whom he had not yet seen clearly—was his brother Tom. But Tom's eyes were a pale blue, not dark gray.

Cushing smiled uncertainly at him. "I reckon he's a man you'll be lookin' forward to meetin'."

Graben nodded again, saying half to himself, "I sure will." Then he gave Cushing a sharper look, and his lips twisted in a cold smile. It was plain that for some reason Knell had Cushing worried, and the fat man had thought of a way to remove the worry, with no cost to himself. Let Graben kill Knell and take the blame for it. And if it worked out the other way around—well, Graben also had Cushing worried. Perhaps even more than Knell did. Perhaps the fat man was hoping Knell would kill him—or better yet, that they would kill each other. Save Cushing and his men the trouble.

"Well, what do you say?" Cushing asked. "You still want to throw in with us? I could use a man like you."

And they were all smiling at him. Even the Kid, whom he had almost begun to like, and who had tried a little while ago to sneak out for coffee water and warn the others he was here.

I'll bet you could, Graben thought. I'll bet you could use a man like me to do your dirty work. Aloud he said, as he holstered his gun and moved toward the table, "That coffee smells good."

Cushing glanced at his men and smiled. He rubbed his plump hands together and laughed at how easy it had been to fool Graben a second time. Then he beamed happily at the clumsy boy who called himself Billy the Kid and said, "Boy, ain't that chuck ready yet?"

The Kid grinned his shy, nervous grin. "Just about."

"Then let's have at it," Cushing said and sank into the nearest chair, almost as tall sitting down as he was standing up. He turned up his sleeves and looked across the table at Graben out of his bright yellow eyes. "You couldn't of come back at a better time. Me and the boys has been thinkin' about something big, and we will need all the help we can get."

"Oh?" Graben said casually, as the Kid filled his tin cup from the smoking coffeepot. "What's that?"

Cushing smiled and watched his face to see how he would react to what he had in mind. "We've been thinkin' about takin' over the Star Ranch," he said. "If we had that ranch, we'd own the basin. We'd own the town. We'd own everything. And instead of bein' two-bit rustlers worryin' all the time about gettin' hung, we'd be big cattlemen."

Graben lit a cigar and smoked it thoughtfully, not offering one to Cushing or the others, turning their expectant smiles to disappointment. "How you plan to go about it?" he asked, his hard face blank.

"It's simple," Cushing said, watching him. "We aim to lure them into a trap and wipe them all out at once—and you're gonna be our bait. As soon as they find out you're here, they'll be comin' after you. And we'll be waitin'."

Graben reached for his cup, his face as unreadable as before. "There's one way to make sure they'll come after me," he said.

"What's that?"

"I'm going after Knell," Graben said. "When I get him, the others will come after me."

Cushing smiled brightly. "Just what I had in mind. With Knell out of the way, the others will be a lot easier to handle." Then he sat there for a moment like a sly fat spider and watched Graben. "But you better take one of the boys with you, just in case. You might need him."

"All right," Graben decided. "I'll take the Kid."

They all stared at him in surprise. "Why the Kid?" Cushing asked.

"I trust him," Graben said.

Graben let his horse rest through the day, and after dark he and the Kid set out. In the first cold gray light of the following dawn, they sat their horses on a rocky ridge a half mile southwest of the vague huddle of buildings and corrals that was the Star headquarters. As they watched, the eastern sky became streaked with red and the buildings stood out more clearly in the growing light. Men could be seen straggling from the bunkhouse to the corral to catch and saddle their horses. A feeble light glowed from the cookshack.

Graben absently felt for a cigar, bit off the end and spat it out. He put the cigar between his teeth but did not light it. He glanced aside at the overgrown boy slumped wearily in the saddle beside him. Graben, accustomed to long rides and scant fare, betrayed no sign of weariness himself, unless it was a certain grim gauntness in his weather-beaten face.

He nodded toward the ranch buildings. "Kid, why don't you ride on down there and tell them you saw me," he said. "When they scatter out hunting me, maybe I can catch Knell by himself."

The Kid shifted uneasily in his saddle. During the long night ride he had been trying to figure out why Graben had picked him for this risky mission. The Kid was not very bright but he did not believe it had anything to do with Graben trusting him. Even he could tell that the tall, bleak-eyed gunfighter trusted no one.

"You mean by myself?"

"Sure, why not?"

The Kid was silent for a time, squirming in his saddle and watching the confused activity at the Star corral. Then he glanced cautiously at Graben out of the corner of one eye. "We ain't had no trouble with them lately," he said. "But I'm afraid if I ride down there by myself they might remember that I'm one of the gang that's been rustlin' their cows."

"Nothing to worry about," Graben said with a bleak smile. "Just tell them you're Billy the Kid and they won't give you any trouble."

Perhaps it was the growing reddish light creeping over the plain from the east that made the Kid's downy cheeks turn red. "I ain't Billy the Kid," he said with a sickly grin. "I reckon you knowed that all along. My name's Harley Cockrell. I only told them rustlers I was Billy the Kid so's they'd let me join up with them. I was afraid they'd laugh in my face if they found out I was just a farm boy from Mississippi."

"I figgered you were a farm boy from somewhere," Graben said, watching the Star hands mount up. "But you don't have to tell them that. Maybe they'll believe you really are Billy the Kid."

Harley Cockrell sighed and seemed to sag in the saddle "I ain't even got a handgun," he said. "You took mine, or the ones I got from Pete. And Mulock's still got my rifle."

Graben scowled for a moment, then reluctantly drew the birdshead Colt from his waistband and handed it to the Kid, butt first. "Here, maybe this will help convince them you're Billy the Kid. I understand he had one like it. I think his had a shorter barrel and ivory or pearl handles, but they won't know the difference."

Harley Cockrell, farm boy from Mississippi, alias Billy the Kid, looked at the gun with interest, then trembled at the thought that he might have to use it. "You sure you won't need it?" he asked.

"Not as much as you will."

That laconic answer did little to reassure the worried youth. He began to sweat, and shoved the gun deep into the waistband of his baggy pants. He looked down toward Star headquarters and squared his shoulders. He tried to sit up straighter in the saddle, but soon began to slump again. "Looks like they're leavin'," he said. "I guess I better git on down there and head them off."

"Good luck," Graben said. "You'll need it."

The Kid reluctantly started his horse down the slope at a plodding walk, slumped over in the saddle like a farm boy on his way home from the field. Graben waited until he had gone twenty feet, then sighed and called him back. The boy eagerly obeyed this time, a big smile revealing his relief and gratitude. They put their horses back over the crest of the ridge and halted again out of sight.

"I've changed my mind," Graben said, frowning at the boy's smile. "You'd likely just tip them off and foul everything up. You better just ride on back a piece where you won't get in the way and wait for me."

"Yes, sir!" Harley Cockrell said eagerly and trotted his horse toward a safer place, Rube Cushing's instructions forgotten.

Graben's lips twisted in mild disgust as he watched the youth slope off. "Billy the Kid," he grunted and spat at the ground. Then he reined his horse back up the slope and halted near the crest where he could watch the approaching riders.

CHAPTER 14

Mark Knell knew something was wrong as they rode toward the rocky ridge painted in the gold and crimson colors of sunrise. The hands were too grim and silent, and three of them—Jud Siskel, Rex Dobler, and Tap Ritchie—lagged back until they were behind him. Graf Stoker glanced back toward the ranch house and then halted the party in the little valley below the ridge. He took time to build a smoke, bent his dark-bearded face over the sudden flare of a match, and said without turning his head, "All right, Jud."

Behind him Knell heard the click of a gun hammer being cocked, and he did not need to look around to know that the gun was pointed at his back. A moment later he heard the whisper of steel on leather as Dobler and Ritchie drew their weapons.

Graf Stoker still did not look at Knell or the three men behind him as he said, "You three stay here with Knell and make sure he don't go nowhere. I don't want him helpin' Graben get away like he did the last time—I don't know why it tuck me so long to figger that out. I ain't decided yet what to do about him, but I don't aim to let him get away with that. Not to mention runnin' his blab to Miss Kate."

"Why don't we just plug him now and be done with it?" Tap Ritchie asked. "Then we can go with y'all. I'd sure like to be there when you find Graben."

"It's a little close to the ranch," Stoker said. "Miss Kate might hear the shot. But I want you to stay where you can see her if she starts toward town. If she does, one of you circle ahead of her and let me know she's comin'."

"You think Graben's still in town?" Jud Siskel asked.

"If he ain't we'll find him, wherever he is," Stoker said grimly, his rough face contorted with hatred. "That bastard ain't gonna get away with what he done."

Mark Knell spoke up at last. "What will Miss Barlow have to say about that?"

Stoker gave him a hard look. "I'll tell her he didn't give us no choice, and this time you won't be around to tell her no different."

"Think she'll believe you?"

"There won't be much she can do about it, even if she don't," Stoker growled and rode off with the rest of the crew, leaving only Knell and his three guards.

Knell waited until Stoker and the others were out of sight, and then he turned carefully in his saddle and looked at the three men holding guns on him—at the long, sparsely bearded face and somber dark eyes of Jud Siskel, at the clean-shaven face and pale green eyes of Tap Ritchie, at the tough, battle-scarred face of Rex Dobler. He saw no cause for reassurance in either of those faces.

"You boys have any idea what you're getting into?" he asked. "Miss Barlow is sure to find out about this, and when she does she'll fire all three of you."

Tap Ritchie's pale green eyes glimmered with hatred. "If she does find out, I don't think it will be you who tells her," he said. "Not this time."

Knell fell silent. They had not taken his gun, and for a moment he wondered about that. Were they thinking about shooting him and then telling Graf Stoker—as well as Kate Barlow—that he had tried to draw on them. It was clear that Ritchie, in particular, wanted to be with the others when they found Graben, and he would jump at any excuse, or perhaps invent one, to dispose of Knell as quickly as possible so he could go on and overtake them.

"All right if I smoke?" Knell asked.

"Go ahead," Siskel told him. "Just be mighty careful with them hands. Tap here is itchin' for an excuse to plug you."

"So I noticed," Knell said, and carefully drew out a slender cigar similar to the kind Graben smoked and lit it.

Rex Dobler looked uneasily over his shoulder toward the ranch house, the shingle roof of which could just be seen from here. "Hadn't we better git around behind that ridge? If Miss Barlow takes a notion to ride into town, she could see us from the road up there."

"She went yesterday," Siskel said. "Ain't likely she'll go back again today. But it won't hurt to take cover in them rocks down there at the foot of the ridge, just in case. You ride ahead, Knell. And keep your right hand on that cigar in your mouth, or it could be the last one you'll ever smoke."

Knell complied in silence, nudging his dark bay toward the jumble of boulders piled up in the bend of the ridge. He studied those rocks uneasily as he approached them. There was no telling how long it might be before Stoker and the others returned, and he did not look forward to spending a long day in those rocks with three armed and possibly trigger-happy men who preferred to be elsewhere. They might decide to shorten the day in a way he would not like.

Of all the hands, Siskel, Ritchie and Dobler were the last three with whom he would have chosen to spend a day in such a place, or any place. He had felt his heart sink a little when Stoker told them to remain with them. For he knew that those three were the least likely to listen to the voice of reason, the least likely to be caught off guard—and the most likely to murder him for any reason or no reason. Undoubtedly, that was the reason why Stoker had chosen them.

They rode around the huge boulders and turned in toward the curving rocky ridge. The battle-scarred Dobler, who seemed to understand better than the other two the kind of man they were dealing with, said quietly, sounding a little nervous, "Hadn't we oughter git his gun?"

Jud Siskel's voice, usually mild and dry, went suddenly hard. "Let him go for it if he wants to. I'm almost hoping he will. I'd sort of like to ride on to town and get there in time for the show. I wouldn't mind putting a few holes in Graben, my own self."

"I'm right here, boys," a quiet deadly voice said, and they looked up to see Graben standing on the rocky slope with a big Russian pistol in his hand. "You don't have to ride all the way to town for your fun."

With a grunt of surprise, Siskel swung his gun toward the tall lean man in black, but he did not swing it fast enough. The Russian pistol exploded like a stick of dynamite and Siskel was blasted out of his saddle.

In one smooth effortless movement Mark Knell swung to the ground drawing his gun and fired over his horse at Tap Ritchie. Ritchie had started to turn his gun on Graben but was swinging it back toward Knell when the latter's bullet caught him high in the chest. An odd look came into his eyes and he seemed to wilt in the saddle before slipping from it to the ground.

In the meantime Rex Dobler, who was left-handed, had snapped a shot at Graben and wheeled his horse to flee, looking back as he fired toward the rocks where Graben stood.

Graben, seemingly in no hurry, stepped to one side, took deliberate aim and fired again. Rex Dobler gave a hoarse cry and toppled off his running horse.

Then Frank Graben and Mark Knell stood staring at one another in silence, each holding a smoking gun in his hand. A day-old stubble of beard darkened Graben's gaunt weathered face; a frown darkened his brow. There was a cold glitter in the narrow faithless gray eyes. The gun in his hand was cocked. By comparison Mark Knell's lean dark face and dark gray eyes, though somber, were serene, composed.

"I've been told it was you put a bullet in me a while back," Graben said.

"Cushing tell you that?"

Graben silently nodded, scowling.

"You believe him?" Knell asked.

Graben shook his head and eased the hammer down on his gun, returned the gun to the cross-draw holster on the left. The gun in the right holster had the butt of the rear for a regular draw, but from what Knell had heard, that gun was rarely used. A faint cold smile twisted Graben's thin lips and he said, "I wouldn't believe anything Cushing told me if he swore on a stack of Bibles."

Knell nodded and put away his own gun, glancing at the three dead men. He sighed. "I'm afraid this means more trouble for you. But I don't guess it matters. Stoker and the others are headed for town looking for you."

Graben's bleak eyes went briefly toward the Star ranch. "That their own idea, or were they just following orders?"

"It was their own idea," Knell said, watching him carefully. "Or Stoker's. Miss Barlow gave him strict orders to let you alone. Somebody in town finally gave her the straight of what happened the night Carl and Shorty were killed."

Graben watched him with a strange look in his eyes for long moment, then asked quietly, "She still think I bushwhacked her pa?"

Knell hesitated. "I think she's about decided that was one of Cushing's boys."

"What does she intend to do about it?" Graben asked.

Knell shrugged. "I don't know. She hasn't told anyone. I don't guess she's decided yet."

Graben again glanced toward the ranch headquarters, then came down the rocky slope and glanced at the dead men. He and Knell were almost exactly the same height and resembled each other a great deal physically. There was a slight facial resemblance as well that could be seen at a glance, though not easily defined. Perhaps that resemblance was just a coincidence, but Knell could not help remembering what Kate Barlow had said.

He smiled faintly now and said, "You've made things sort of uncomfortable for me in more ways than one. I've even been accused of being your brother."

Graben studied him for a moment and then said, "I've only got one brother as far as I know, and you don't look much like I remember him."

Knell shrugged. "I haven't got any, as far as I know. My old man cut out before I was born. Turned out he was one of a bunch of Missouri raiders who came over to Kansas and caused some trouble. That was three or four years before the border wars really got started. I don't think there were supposed to be any settlers in that part of Kansas in 1850, but there were some anyway and they were already talking about making it a free state. Seems some folks over in Missouri heard about it and didn't like it, so they came over and raised some hell. My old man was with them and he got shot up pretty bad. My mother found him and took care of him and one thing led to another, I guess. But he got drunk one night and told the wrong person about being one of the Missouri bunch and some men came looking for him. He disappeared and I never saw him. I don't know whether he went back to Missouri or what happened to him."

Graben listened with interest, betraying some surprise, but then shook his head with confidence. "My old man used to talk about raising some hell over in Kansas. Seems like he mentioned getting shot over there. But he sure never said anything about having a wife over there—and he would have been sure to tell someone and I would have heard about it. He wasn't much like me and Tom in that respect—he never could keep anything to himself."

Knell shrugged. "Well, I wasn't looking for a long lost brother anyway. I wouldn't know what to do if I found one."

Graben sighed. "I've got a long lost brother somewhere, if he's still alive—and I wouldn't know what to do or say if I ran into him. I ain't seen him in ten years." Then he asked, "I don't guess you ever ran into a Tom Graben in your travels?"

Knell shook his head. "Not as far as I know."

Graben was silent for a time, gazing bleakly off into the distance. He was like that when he said, "I don't guess you'd happen to know who hauled me to that old prospector's shack while I was unconscious with that bullet in my carcass?"

Knell was also gazing into the distance. "I couldn't say."

Graben turned and looked at him directly. "I told Cushing I was going to kill you," he said. "He seemed to think that would bring the other hands chasing me into an ambush he'd have ready for them. That's what he said anyway. But I've got a feeling it's me he's planning to ambush."

"That could be," Knell agreed. After a moment he said, almost reluctantly, "I'm pretty sure Cushing has made some kind of deal with Stoker."

Graben looked at him sharply. "What kind of deal?"

"I think Stoker has agreed to let them alone if Cushing will give him a cut of the money from the cattle they run off."

"Any of the other Star hands in on it?"

Knell nodded at the dead bodies. "I'm pretty sure those three were. I could be wrong, but I don't much think any of the other hands know about it. Not yet anyway."

"What about Kate Barlow? Does she know about it?"

"I don't think so," Knell said. "I've thought about telling her, but I'm a little uneasy about what might happen. She'd fire Stoker, and then it wouldn't surprise me if he didn't get some of the hands and run off all her stock, or even try to take over the ranch. He acts like he owns it already."

Graben looked at him through his doomed gray eyes and asked quietly, "You think it would help if I killed him? One more won't make much difference to me one way or the other."

Knell seemed to consider it for a moment, then said carefully, "I've sort of taken a personal interest in Stoker myself. I know he's got to be stopped, but I figure it's my place to stop him. Then I guess it will be about time for me to ride on. If I stay here there will be trouble with the other hands, and that would just mean more trouble for Miss Barlow."

Graben's eyes seemed to get bleaker at the mention of her name, but his hard face remained blank. He nodded and, unexpectedly, held out is hand. "Well, Knell, I wish you luck. If I didn't already have a brother I wouldn't mind adopting you. But I figger one brother's all any man can rightly cope with."

Knell smiled and took the hand briefly. "I figure one is probably more than I could cope with."

A very bleak smile, more like a shadow than light, passed briefly over Graben's own craggy face. "Especially if it was me, you mean."

About a mile from the ridge Graben found the Kid waiting for him. The Kid was grinning like he expected an old friend.

"I'm surprised to see you," Graben said, reining in. "I figgered you'd be halfway back to Cushing's shack by now. Or maybe on your way back to Mississippi."

"I been sort of thinkin' about how nice it'd be to go back home," the Kid admitted sheepishly. "I've about decided I ain't cut out to be no outlaw."

"It sure took you long enough," Graben said. "I knew that the first time I set eyes on you."

The Kid blinked in wonder. "You did?"

"Sure," Graben said, lighting a cigar. "I could tell you didn't belong with that bunch."

The Kid sighed and folded his hands on the saddle horn. "I reckon it's been plain all along to ever'body but me."

"Do yourself a favor, Kid," Graben told him. "Go on back home while you can and forget about being an outlaw. There's no future in it. I'd go back home in a minute if I could."

"You would?"

"Sure," Graben said. "Most fellows like me would, if they had a home to go back to and weren't afraid the law might be watching the house. You'll find yourself in that fix if you wait too long."

"I been sort of thinkin' about goin' back," the Kid said.

"Don't think about it," Graben said. "Do it. Go home and see your folks, while they're still around."

The Kid sat there bent over in his saddle thinking about it and his homely face lit up in a grin that became toothier and toothier the more he thought about it. He sat up straighter in the saddle and pulled his old slouch hat down more securely on his head to withstand the wind of fast riding. "By God, I believe I will," he said.

Graben nodded. "A smart decision. Smarter than you'll ever

know."

Harley Cockrell whooped with the relief of leaving danger behind him and the joy of going home to watermelon and home cooking and smiling familiar faces. He started riding off, then reined in and asked, "You want yore gun back?"

"You keep it," Graben told him. "Someday you can tell your grandkids that Billy the Kid gave it to you."

Harley Cockrell grinned, then thought for a moment and shook his head. "No, I reckon I'll tell them Frank Graben give it to me, along with some good advice."

Chapter 15

Mrs. Wilkins stood with her bare feet braced apart, blocking the door of the squatter shack. "What do you want here?" she demanded. Like she had a right to be there and they didn't, they said later.

The tall bearded Star foreman had dismounted and was striding toward the door, out of the afternoon sun into the shadow of the house. The others remained in their saddles, hoping to catch a glimpse of the red-haired girl past the stout, frowning squatter woman, whom they resented for being there, obstructing the view and evidently intending to obstruct any attempted entrance into the shack. Just like it was hers, and they would have put her and Wilkins out a long time ago if it had not been for the girl.

"Where's Wilkins?" Stoker asked.

"He went to town."

Stoker scowled. "Funny we never saw him," he said. "We just came from there."

"Well, that's where he said he was goin'."

He did not believe her and his rough bearded face showed it. "Frank Graben been around here?" he asked.

"We ain't seen nobody," she said, not wanting to get involved in any trouble.

Stoker made an impatient gesture. "Send that red-haired girl up to tell Cushing I want to see him," he said. "I meant to send Wilkins, but if he ain't here I'll have to send her."

"Go tell him yourself," Mrs. Wilkins said. "Or send one of your men."

Stoker took a deep breath. His voice shook with anger. "Don't you try my patience, woman. I been meanin' to put y'all off Star range now for quite a while, and that's just what I'll do if you give me any trouble."

"Knock her teeth out, Graf," one of the hands said, laughing. "Kick her in the belly."

Ignoring him, Stoker asked, "You aim to do like I say or not?"

For a long moment she stood glaring at him, showing no fear and a great deal of anger and dislike. Then she closed the door in his face and turned to look at her daughter, who sat pale and trembling in a chair. "I guess you better ride up there and tell Cushing what he said," Mrs. Wilkins said. "I reckon you'll be about as safe goin' up there as stayin' here, with them around. But you go straight up there and back, you hear. And don't get off the horse. Just tell Cushing that Graf Stoker wants to see him and then hurry on back. I'll try to get rid of this bunch while you're gone."

It was late afternoon when Graben tied his horse in a juniper thicket and began making his way cautiously through the trees and rocks on foot. On his way back he had avoided the trail, although he thought he knew where Cushing's men would be waiting for him—behind a natural breastwork of rocks at the top of a long slope.

And he was right. From some brush he soon saw Lum Mulock and Paris France standing behind the rocks facing downslope, with rifles cradled in their arms, smoking and talking and laughing about something. Those two seemed to find everything funny. He wondered how funny they would find his sudden appearance from the wrong direction, when he stepped into the open and they saw him.

The afternoon had been hot, but now a cool breeze stirred through the pinons and junipers, sighing down the long slope where the trees were more scattered, soon giving way to scrub cedar. It was an ideal spot for an ambush—and if Graben did not miss his guess, it was where Whitey Barlow had been killed.

The fact that only Mulock and France were here was proof that Graben, and not the entire Star crew, was the intended victim this time. Cushing had told him that they would all be here armed for bear, waiting for him to ride up. Then they would all wait for the Star riders and wipe them out before they knew what hit them. But

Graben had not believed that any of the time, for it had seemed far too reckless and risky for a man as cautious and crafty, as fond of his own fat carcass, as Cushing. And his hunch had been right. At the present time Cushing wanted only two men eliminated—Graben and Mark Knell, both of whom had him worried for some reason. Well, his worries were not over, if he only knew it. Not yet.

Graben's lips twisted with scorn at the thought of the fat rustler waiting back in his shack for word that he, Graben, was dead, but keeping his top gunhand, Pete Lutter, with him just in case.

The expression of scorn on Graben's face deepened presently at the antics of Mulock and France who, instead of watching for him, had lapsed into horseplay more suitable for schoolboys than professional outlaws. They were feinting and thrusting with their rifles as if they had bayonets attached to them, and the clang of metal on metal could have been heard for quite a distance.

They were both grinning from ear to ear and so absorbed in their fun that they did not see the red-haired girl coming up the slope on the gaunt work horse. She rode astride, without a saddle, and her old skirt was pulled up on slender but shapely white legs. When Graben saw her he lowered his gun and stepped back farther into the brush and rocks.

Mulock and France did not see her until she was almost to the top of the hill. Then they broke off their horseplay with the rifles and turned sweaty, beaming faces toward her. "Well, look what we got here," Mulock said with a broad grin. And she was smiling back as she rode up and halted the bony nag. Watching from his concealment, Graben was puzzled to see on her smooth white face none of the fear she had shown the two times he had seen her. She had gotten used to the rustlers who were frequent visitors at the squatter shack. She had even come to enjoy their good-natured fun and the fuss they made over her, never realizing what went on in their minds or what they said behind her back. She did not notice the sly glance Mulock and France exchanged now. She did not realize this was the moment they had been waiting for, when they would have her alone, away from her stout sharp-eyed mother.

"What you doin' way off up here, Molly girl?" Mulock asked, catching hold of the bridle.

A look of worry darkened the girl's eyes as she remembered her mission. "Ma sent me," she said. "That Graf Stoker and his men are down at the shack and they wanted me to come up here and tell Mr.

Cushing they want to see him. I had to come, 'cause Pa went off to town or someplace."

"Why didn't Stoker come hisself?" Mulock asked. Then his grin broadened. "Not that we wouldn't ruther see you."

The girl smiled as if pleased, looking down at him with trusting eyes. "He didn't say. But I think he's afraid to come up here after what happened to Whitey Barlow. I guess he's afraid Graben might shoot him too."

"Could be," Mulock said and exchanged another grin with the silent Paris France.

"Well, I'm glad I saw y'all here," the girl said. "Now I won't have to go on up to the shack, if y'all will tell Mr. Cushing what I said. Ma wanted me to hurry back as quick as I could. She'll be worried sick about me."

"What's the hurry?" Mulock asked, getting a better grip on the bridle strap. The toothy grin began to look frozen on his swarthy round face. "This is the first time you ever come up here and you want to go back before you even got here good!"

The girl's own smile became a little strained and uncomfortable. "It's because of Ma," she said. "She starts worrying every time I get out of her sight."

"There ain't nothin' to worry about," Mulock said in an odd voice. "At least get down and rest a little. There's plenty of nice shady spots around here."

The girl glanced about the forest with a shadow of dread in her dark eyes, and seemed to sense what the rustlers had in mind. "No, I really have to get back," she said with a tremor in her voice.

"Aw, come on now," the chunky man said, reaching up to pull her off the tired horse and laughing to make it seem like it was all in fun and there was nothing to worry about. France eagerly helped him and they dragged the alarmed, protesting girl under a nearby tree. Still grinning, pretending that they were just playing with her—a little wrestling match—they held her down on her back and began running their hands over her body. Becoming more excited, Mulock suddenly ripped her blouse open and she screamed and attempted to cover the exposed area with her folded arms.

Graben stood twenty feet away with a gun in his hand, his jaws clenched in anger. But they did not see him until he said in a cold deadly tone, "Mulock."

Red-faced and sweating, his swarthy features contorted with

lust, Mulock looked around at him in surprise. He saw the cold glitter of hatred in Graben's eyes, the gun in his fist, and his own eyes widened with terror. He released the girl and reached for his gun. Graben shot him between the eyes. The girl screamed as if she had been shot. Then Graben turned the gun on Paris France who was scrambling frantically away, clawing at his own gun. Graben's pistol roared again and the man with the sly twisted face was slammed to the ground. He tried to push himself up but his trembling arms collapsed under him and he did not move after that.

The terror-stricken girl was also scrambling away, trying to pull the torn pieces of her blouse over what Graben had already glimpsed. For such a scrawny looking little thing she was surprisingly well developed. He would remember those plump white breasts, and think about them now and then, until the day he died. But he would also remember the fear on her white face and in her dark eyes as she ran away down the slope, looking back over her shoulder. She still seemed more afraid of him than she had been of Mulock and France even when they were attacking her. It was some instinctive dread of the killer in him.

He laughed and shook his head, partly in amazement, perhaps partly to show his scorn and resentment. "Hadn't you better take your horse?" he called after her. "It's a long walk back home, especially without any shoes." But he reflected that she was probably used to going barefoot, like most nester girls.

She ran on a piece and then slowed to a stop, holding the torn blouse together over her heaving breasts. Her voice was unsteady and husky with excitement as she said, "You go away first!"

Still chuckling and shaking his head in wonder, he moved farther away from the half-dead work horse that had not even raised its drooping head during all the excitement, being used to the noise of guns and the craziness of humans. The girl kept her wide eyes on him as she carefully approached the horse, then she turned her back to him as she quickly swung astride the animal's bare back. As soon as she was mounted, one hand went back to the torn blouse, and her dark eyes went to the two dead men. A look of anguish and horror twisted her pale face.

"Now what do you think of your fun-loving friends?" Graben asked.

She looked at him with dread in her eyes, then turned the old horse around and kicked it into feeble motion back down the slope.

She glanced quickly over her shoulder as if to make sure he was not
following her, and then she remembered something and called, "Tell
Mr. Cushing that Graf Stoker wants to see him down at our place!"
Apparently she thought Graben had joined back up with the gang, as
indeed he had pretended to.

He shrugged. "I'll tell him. But I don't think he'll be able to come."

She looked at him uncertainly and then rode on down the slope,
urging the bony old horse to a shambling trot. Graben looked after
her until she was out of sight, the silent humorless laughter turning sour inside him. His weathered face became grim and bleak. He
reloaded his gun, then got the pistols that the two dead men had
dropped and shoved them in his waistband. He did not bother with
the rifles. He had not used a rifle in so long that one felt awkward
in his hands. And he did not think he would need a rifle for the job
ahead. He wanted to be close enough to see the shock and fear on
their faces when he shot them.

He returned to his horse and rode on toward the rustler shack, de-
scending into a cedar-dotted valley half a mile wide and then climbing again into the pinons and junipers. He circled around and left his
horse on the rough, rocky slope above the house where he had left it
two nights before. The slope and the shack below were in shadow,
but the sinking sun crowned the higher trees with gold. There were
a few scattered pines toward the top of the slope, towering above the
pinons and junipers.

On foot now, Graben made his way down the dark gray slope with
what might have seemed a careless disregard for safety, had anyone
seen him. But no one did. Pete Lutter, at the shack window, was
watching in the other direction for Mulock and France to return with
the happy news that Graben was dead. And Cushing was absorbed
in a game of solitaire at the plank table, studying his cards with a
look of gloating satisfaction on his fat round face, as if he had just
discovered a new way to cheat.

"Reckon I better feed and water the horses 'fore it gets dark,"
Lutter said. Cushing did not seem to hear him, and after a moment
the lanky rustler opened the creaky door and stepped outside into
the cool evening breeze coming down off the mountains. He started
leisurely across the hard-packed ground toward the corral, carrying
his rifle in one hand with the muzzle down.

From the corner of the shack Graben said quietly, "Lutter."

Pete Lutter turned and saw the tall dark gunfighter standing there casually with his left shoulder against the corner of the shack, his right hand resting lightly on the stag handle of Paris France's Colt in his waistband.

Lutter swung the rifle up—the same rifle with which he had shot Graben from ambush five months ago. He saw the gleam of blue steel as Paris France's fancy new Colt whipped out of Graben's waistband. He saw the muzzle jump and flash in the purple twilight and heard the roar as the lead bit into him. As he dropped the rifle and fell he saw the merciless glitter in Graben's narrow gray eyes and the scowling dark brows over them.

Then Graben stepped quickly to the shack window, broke the glass with the Colt barrel and fired in the same movement.

Cushing, lurching up out of his chair and grabbing for his gun, took the bullet in his fat belly and sat back down with a huge grunt, a look of bewildered surprise and agony spreading slowly over his face. The gun slipped from his fingers and clattered to the floor.

A moment later Graben kicked the door open and stepped inside with the stag-handled Colt cocked and ready. He walked around the table, kicked Cushing's gun across the floor, and stood behind him for a silent moment. The fat man sat motionless in the chair holding his belly with both hands and did not turn his head. Graben went back around to the other side of the table and stood facing the fat man. Cushing watched him with worried eyes but remained silent.

"What's wrong, Cushing?" Graben taunted. "All of a sudden you don't look too happy. Something didn't work out the way you planned?"

Cushing still said nothing. His eyes avoided Graben's cold gray stare.

Graben suddenly threw the stag-handled Colt aside, leaned over the table and slapped the rustlers's fat round face.

Baffled, Cushing gaped up at him and cried, "What did you do that for?"

"I just wanted to make sure I still had your attention," Graben said. "That squatter girl wanted me to give you a message. She said Graf Stoker wanted to see you down at their shack. I told her I didn't think you'd be able to make it." He lit a cigar, watching the fat rustler, who had again lapsed into silence, sweat beading his round face as he sat there in the fading light trying to hold his guts in. "But I'm curious, Rube. What do you think Graf Stoker wanted to see you about? I thought you and him were old enemies. Maybe I was wrong, eh? Maybe a lot of people were wrong."

Cushing sat silent. Then, still holding his belly, he slowly fell sideways out of his chair, and lay motionless on his side, doubled up in pain, staring at Graben's legs under the table, at the dusty black boots. After a little silence the boots and the long legs turned and went slowly toward the door.

"Well, so long, Cushing. Try to enjoy the next hour or two. That's all the time you've got left."

Graben left the shack and started across the yard to the corral to turn the horses out. The rustlers would not need them anymore. Hearing a sudden racket in the shack, he turned to find Cushing at the window with a gun in his hand. Once again he had underestimated the fat rustler.

Graben had carried the birdshead Colt in his waistband so long that his hand now darted for it automatically, and closed on the walnut stock of Lum Mulock's .45. He jerked up the heavy Colt and thumbed a shot at the window just as Cushing was getting set to fire. The big rustler's plump face seemed to collapse as the bullet smashed his Adam's apple. His gun dropped outside the window and he fell back out of sight and crashed to the floor like a heavy log.

Graben stood rigid with the gun trained on the window. But now there was silence in the shack and he knew Cushing was dead. Turning away he tossed Mulock's gun aside and went on to the corral to free the horses.

Chapter 16

Knell knocked on the door a little after dark and heard her voice—it sounded a little uncertain and uneasy, which was not at all like her. She had always seemed composed and sure of herself almost to the point of arrogance.

"Who is it?"

"Knell."

There was a quick patter of feet, the door opened and she stood in the dim lamplight peering anxiously at the shadow of his face under his black hat. He suddenly got the feeling that she had been waiting, hoping he could come, because she had come to depend on him in some way. And the thought made him uneasy. It made what he had come to tell her that much harder—that he had to go, that it was a mistake for him to be here even now. But he could not leave without offering some explanation, for he owed her that much, and he did not want to go away thinking she might believe whatever the others decided to tell her.

"Come in," she said. "I was hoping you would come." She sounded a little breathless, almost frightened—but not of him, of something else. She retreated to the center of the room and turned to watch him step inside and close the door softly behind him, thoughtfully removing his hat. With anxious eyes she studied his grave dark face and seemed even more disturbed by his silence, as he groped for the right words. She spoke again, unable to contain her curiosity and worry.

"What was that shooting about this morning?"

He sighed wearily. "It's sort of a long story." And there was no time for long stories. Graf Stoker and the crew might ride up at any moment, and he did not want them to find him here. There was no sense endangering her.

She watched him silently for a moment, and then spoke softly, almost as if she were afraid someone else might be listening, though she was alone in the house. "I thought about going out there to see what it was all about. But I decided it might not be a good idea. The way things are now, I'm almost afraid to know about some of the things that go on around here. It might not be safe to know too much."

He nodded, understanding what she meant. "What you need is a new foreman and a new crew. I don't think any of the men you've got now can be trusted too far. That's why I waited until dark to come here—I'm not even sure I can trust the cook. But your biggest problem at the moment is Graf Stoker. If he was out of the way and you had a new foreman, a man you could rely on, then you could start thinking about replacing any of the hands who gave you trouble."

"Do you have anyone in mind?" she asked, watching him with her direct green eyes.

He shook his head. "Not at the moment."

"I thought you might take the job," she said. "I've about decided you're the only one I can trust."

He looked at her in surprise, then again shook his head. "I'm about the last man in the world for the job."

"What makes you say that?"

He sighed. "Maybe I better tell you what happened out there this morning." He kept it as brief as possible, and finished by adding, "When they find out what happened, they'll be looking for me and Graben too. That's why I can't stay here, let alone take the foreman's job. That's what I came to tell you."

A stillness settled over her rather strong but beautiful face, making it seem older. A light faded from her green eyes. When she spoke her voice was quiet, composed. "When are you leaving?"

"Tonight. No later than tomorrow." He hesitated. "I don't guess I'll see you again. But I'll be watching for the sort of man you need for a foreman and I'll tell him there's a vacancy here."

"If there isn't now," she said, her green eyes turning chilly, "there soon will be."

"Yes," he agreed, "there soon will be."

It was well past midnight when Stoker and the others halted their tired horses at the foot of the dark ridge and peered up at the rocks. "Jud," the bearded foreman called quietly.

There was no answer, and one of the hands said, "They prob'ly went on back to the ranch."

"Jud," Stoker said again, louder this time.

"He can't here you," Knell said. "You'll find him and the other two down there at the bend in the ridge."

They sat up straighter in their saddles, suddenly wide awake where they had been half asleep a moment before, and their eyes searched the rocks. It took them only a moment to spot his dark hat and gleaming pistol—about all that showed above the rock. Stoker grabbed for his own gun and had it half out of the holster when Knell's voice stopped him.

"Go ahead. I've been hoping you would."

The big foreman froze, his elbow bent, the gun still only half drawn. He sat that way for a moment, as if turned to stone in the act of drawing. Then he let out a long breath and let the gun slide back in the holster, moving his hand away from it.

"Tell the others to go on to the ranch," Knell said.

Stoker peered uneasily up at the shadowy outline of his face under the dark hat. "What you got in mind?" the big man asked hoarsely.

"You and I are going to have a little talk," Knell said. "In private. If any of the others try sneaking back before we're finished, I'm liable to take it out on you."

"Rest of you go on ahead," Stoker said gruffly. "I'll be along before long. If I ain't—" He did not finish, but somehow his meaning was clear.

The others silently turned their horses and rode on toward the ranch at a walk, looking back toward the rocks. Knell was silent also as he watched them go.

"Start talkin'," Stoker told him impatiently, his anger overriding his fear. "I ain't got all night."

"That's right," Knell told him. "You ain't got all night. You've only got as much time as I decide to give you."

Stoker's bearded face darkened in a scowl. "What's that supposed to mean?" he grunted.

For a time Knell was silent, again watching the Star riders until they vanished into the dark huddle of buildings a half mile away. Then he turned his attention back to the big man sitting impatiently in his saddle at the foot of the ridge.

"Stoker," he said, "what do you think would happen if I killed you?"

The foreman stiffened. Then he said, "The hands would come after you. They'd hunt you down."

"That's just what I was thinking," Knell agreed. "They'll come after me and follow me as long as I leave a trail they can follow. That will give Graben plenty of time to wind up his business here and get out of the country. By the time they get back they will be too worn out from chasing me to be in any mood or any shape to go after him."

It was Stoker's turn to be silent. The expression of his dark-bearded face was hidden by the shadow of his hat. He might have been thinking any number of things. He might have been thinking that Knell's horse was fresh while those of the Star hands were worn out and it would take them a while to round up some more. He might have been remembering Knell's uncanny ability to leave no trail when it suited his purpose. The hands would be able to follow his trail only as long as he wanted them to follow it, and no farther. Or the burly foreman might have been trying to think of some way to save his own hide. It would not be unlike him to think of himself first.

In any case, he seemed sunk in thought. But presently he was startled back to alertness by the sound of boots crunching on gravel. His shaggy head snapped up and he saw Knell coming down through the rocks to stand about fifteen feet in front of the horse, facing him. He saw that Knell had holstered his gun, and the breath hissed through his teeth as his heart began to pound. Here was his chance. Maybe a slim one, but it was the only chance he had. He took it. His hand clawed at his gun. Before he could get it out, Knell's gun flashed and roared, blasting him into hell.

Graben got back to town early the next morning, checked into the hotel and slept until midafternoon. By then Jill Dauber had washed and dried and pressed his clothes—all of them except the brown corduroy coat. He was awakened by her knock on the door.

"Your clothes are ready, Frank," she called. "What do you want me to do with them?"

"Bring them on in," he said. "The door's not locked."

She opened the door and came in with the clothes on hangers, a look of surprise on her face. She hung the clothes on a nail in the wall and turned to regard him with her faded eyes. She patted her gray-streaked hair into place with an unconscious gesture and said, "You're getting sort of careless, aren't you?"

He nodded, clasping his hands behind his head on the pillow and watching her through his still gray eyes. After a moment his lips twisted in a faint smile. "I always sort of wanted to die in bed," he said. "Just go to sleep and never wake up. It wouldn't be such a bad way to go. There's just one thing wrong with the idea."

"What's that?"

She saw his gray eyes turning cold again, and tried not to show her disappointment. For a moment he had seemed almost human. "If I die in bed anytime soon," he said, "it will be because somebody blasted the daylights out of me. And that's a fellow I'd sure like to take with me." Then he glanced at the door and asked, "Where's Dauber? I didn't see him when I came in."

She sat down on the edge of the bed almost as if giving way to the weariness that suddenly showed in her face. "Apparently he left," she said.

"Left?" Graben echoed in surprise.

She nodded, then laughed nervously. "All these years I've been thinking about leaving him, and now he's left me. I think he was afraid if he stayed here you'd kill him. He knew he couldn't control himself when he got to drinking, and he couldn't let it alone, so he decided to leave before he got himself killed. But I imagine he'll sneak back when he knows you're gone for good." She turned her head and gave him a worried glance. "Or dead."

"That reminds me of something you said the night I left," he said. "You were going to tell me something when I got back."

"Oh, I was going to warn you," she said. "Sam told me, in that sneering sarcastic way he's got when he's been drinking, that I might as well forget about you, because you would be dead pretty soon. It wasn't much trouble to get it out of him what he meant by that. He said that Max Rumford, Hiram Goodman and Barney Ludlow had decided to kill you. He wanted in on it, but they knew he couldn't be relied on because of his drinking."

"You mean that storekeeper was in on it?" Graben asked.

She nodded. "They cut cards to see which one would try to get you first. I'm not sure whose turn it is next, whether it's Max Rumford or Barney Ludlow. But you better watch out for both of them."

"They better watch out for me," Graben said, an icy glitter in his eyes. "I figgered all along those two were out to get me, but I sure never thought Hiram Goodman would have the guts to try something like that."

Jill Dauber gave a scornful little laugh. "There's a lot about Hiram Goodman you don't know," she said. "That wasn't even his real name. It was Hiram Peabody before he changed it."

"Peabody!" Graben echoed. He was surprised that his guess had been right even though he doubted it himself.

She nodded. "I shouldn't tell you this, but I don't guess it matters now, and I don't think you'll repeat it to anyone. Hiram used to work in a bank in Chicago. We lived there then and so did Max Rumford and Barney Ludlow. Sam and Max and Barney were old war buddies, and we had a small account at the bank where Hiram worked, so we soon became acquainted with him. Well, times were hard—it was the panic of '73—and they got to thinking about all that money in the bank. It was easy to persuade Hiram to go in with them because he'd sort of lost his head over me."

"I'll be damned!" Graben said. "I was right! I didn't even believe it myself, but I was right! I remembered seeing an old picture in a newspaper years ago that reminded me of Goodman. One night I played a little prank on him, threatening to tell everyone he was Peabody. I thought he was afraid the story would ruin his name even though it wasn't true. But it really was true after all."

Jill Dauber seemed delighted to see the gloomy gunfighter smiling and animated, so unlike his usual self. She eagerly laughed with him and said, "He was a funny little man in a lot of ways. He tried for years to get me to run away with him. I suppose I'm the cause of his ruin, but I never encouraged him. I always did my best to discourage him, but it never seemed to do any good."

There was a little silence. When she turned her head and looked at Graben she saw that his smile had faded. His eyes had become bleak and cold again—and distant. His thoughts had strayed away. And her own smiled faded and her eyes grew worried as she watched him.

"I probably shouldn't have told you about Max and Barney," she said. "Now I guess you'll have to go after them. But I felt I had to warn you. I knew they wouldn't give you a chance if they could help it."

Graben did not answer. He did not seem to hear her. The icy glitter was back in his eyes.

A short time later Graben, wearing his black clothes and Russian pistols, crossed the street to the barbershop and stretched out in the chair.

"I remember how you want it cut," the pink-skinned little barber said. "You don't want it to look like it was cut at all."

"Just a shave," Graben said.

"I see." The pink-skinned barber put away his scissors and comb and began stropping his razor. "I think I've finally figgered out who was in the alley that night," he said over his shoulder. "It was that little Shorty guy."

"Think so?"

"I'd be willing to swear to it. Now that he's dead. But don't tell the other hands I said that. They'd skin me alive with my own razor, and enjoy doing it too. I never saw a meaner crew in my whole life. And Graf Stoker wouldn't lift a finger to stop them."

Graben was silent. His cold gray eyes were looking through the window at the saloon across the street.

Ten minutes later he rose from the chair, pushing away the mirror the little barber held up before his clean-shaven face. He put on his black hat, handed the barber a quarter, and silently left the barbershop.

He crossed the street to the saloon and slowly went in through the swing doors. The place was dim and empty. Max Rumford stood behind the bar like a two-legged bull in a white shirt, turned sideways to watch him come in. Graben adjusted his hat as he stepped up to the bar about eight feet from the saloonkeeper. He did not seem to notice the dull hostility in the big man's bloodshot eyes. Rumford wordlessly slid a bottle and a glass down the bar to him. Graben uncorked the bottle and poured himself a drink.

"I hear you and Ludlow plan to kill me," he said almost casually.

Max Rumford became utterly motionless behind the bar, glaring silently at him through the bloodshot eyes. Graben looked at him now and his own eyes were a little colder than usual, if that was possible.

"Who's turn is it next?" he asked. "Yours or Ludlow's?"

Rumford's face became congested with blood. He looked as if he were slowly choking on something he could not swallow. "Mine," he almost whispered.

"Then I guess I came to the right place," Graben said.

Rumford did not say anything.

Graben stared at him with bitter eyes. "When I think how easy you bastards could have avoided trouble with me," he said. "All I wanted was a little peace and quiet."

Rumford still did not say anything. He looked a little embarrassed. Perhaps he finally realized the mistake he had made, the mistake they had all made, now when it was too late.

"Well, when a man sets out to kill me I always give him a chance to try," Graben said, with a hint of sarcasm in his tone. He was silent a moment, watching Rumford. Then he asked, "You got a scattergun under there?"

Rumford slowly nodded.

"Bring it out and put it on the bar," Graben said.

After a long moment the saloonkeeper slowly reached for the sawed-off shotgun and laid it carefully on the bar, as he had been told to do. The twin muzzles just happened to be pointed down the bar in Graben's direction.

Then the saloonkeeper watched with interest as Graben slowly drew one of his Russians from the holster and placed it on the bar. "I guess that should even things up," the gunfighter said.

Rumford stood gazing down at the shotgun for a long moment with tormented eyes. A look of anguish spread over his homely face. He looked as if he wanted to weep and beg Graben to let him off. But he could not bring himself to do it.

Then with what sounded almost like a sob he reached for the shotgun.

There was a single shot in the saloon, and the town waited, watching the front of the saloon through cracks and curtained windows. The town did not have long to wait. A minute later the tall black-garbed gunfighter came out of the saloon and strode down the street toward the livery stable.

Barney Ludlow was waiting in the barn loft with his Winchester and a pint bottle of whiskey he had been saving for emergencies. When he saw Graben leave the saloon and start down the street he took a long drink from the bottle, wiped his mouth, then wiped his sweaty hands on his overalls and got a better grip on the rifle. His heart was pounding wildly and the sweat was pouring into his eyes so that he could barely see through the narrow crack in the plank wall. He frantically wiped his eyes, raised the rifle and tried to get a bead on Graben through the crack. But from the back end of the Winchester he could not even see the tall gunfighter striding down the street!

On his knees he walked over to the gable door and sighted down the barrel at Graben when the latter was no more than twenty feet away. He had Graben right in his sights and he was taking up the slack on the trigger, his sweaty face shining and contorted with gloating triumph. By then Graben had seen him of course, but it was too late. The man's goose was cooked. He would scare no one else with his pretense of being a gunfighter.

And then the impossible happened. Graben flipped up a gun and fired before Ludlow could finish taking up the slack on the trigger, and the bullet turned Ludlow sideways so that his own shot went wide. And then he lost his balance and cried out as he felt himself falling.

He hit the ground with a heavy thud that probably broke every bone in his body, and to add insult to injury he saw Graben standing as tall and dark as a cloud above him, shutting out the sun.

"Don't worry, Graben," he managed to hiss with his last breath. "Sooner or later you'll get yours."

Graben bared his teeth in a wolfish grin. "I'll settle for later." In truth he no longer cared much when it happened, but he did not want Barney Ludlow to know that. He did not want anyone to know it. Perhaps that at least was one secret he could carry to his grave.

He saddled the blue roan and rode up the street to the hotel, got down and went inside. Jill Dauber was in the lobby, her eyes stricken, a numb look on her face. She silently watched him climb the stairs and showed no surprise when he came back down a few minutes later with his saddlebags and blanket roll.

"You don't have to leave," she said, though she knew it was no use. "Sam won't come back until he knows you're gone. He may not come back at all."

"I'm not leaving because of Sam," he said. "I'm leaving because of me."

And she knew he would not take her with him for the same reason. Because he was Frank Graben, and there was an emptiness inside him that she could never fill. An emptiness that no woman could fill, except perhaps one. And she was not the one.

She sighed and almost collapsed in a chair. Her eyes were dry but she was crying inside. She sat there and did not get up and go the window even when she heard his horse trotting slowly up the street and out of town. She did not want to watch another man ride out of her life.

Thank you for reading
The Return of Frank Graben
by Van Holt.

We hope you enjoyed this story. If so, please leave a review about your experience so others may discover Van Holt.

You may also enjoy another story about some famous gunfighters called *The Hellbound Man*

Excerpt from
The Hellbound Man
by Van Holt

Jim Benton was riding another lonely trail which he knew would soon lead him to more trouble, if it led anywhere. But it did not really matter. He was past thirty and past caring. He had already lived longer than he had expected to.

He wore dark clothes and rode a dark horse. The horse was dark brown but most people would have called it a black horse. Benton's hair was dark brown with a copper or reddish tinge, but most people would have said it was black, and under the frowning dark brows his gray eyes often looked black too. Whatever Benton wore looked black on him. But he never wore light-colored clothes. They were too easily seen, made too good a target.

He was a tall lean man with a strength in his arms and shoulders that was not apparent at first glance. But there were taller and stronger men, and somewhere there was a man who was faster with a gun, or one who would put a bullet in his back. Every step along the trail brought him that much closer to such a man. But he could not stop and he could not turn back. He had to keep going.

A barren desert waste lay behind him and there was more desert country ahead, but now the trail led through scattered tall pines where there was little undergrowth. Here and there boulders or rock outcrops could be seen through the trees.

It was late in the year and rather cold in the shade. But here and there he rode through patches of warm sunlight, and occasional meadows where nothing grew but brown grass and a few scattered pines. Good cattle country, but he saw no cattle.

Around a bend of the trail he caught sight of a wagon stopped in a little clearing. The middle-aged man with the lines in his hands turned a frank friendly face to smile at him and asked, "Where you bound, stranger?"

"Hell, I guess," Benton said before he noticed the two girls on the seat beside the man. He stopped the brown gelding and asked, "Trouble?"

"No, just lettin' the horses blow," the man said. "Been pushin' them right along. Want to get back to Rustler's Roost. I believe somebody named the town that as a bad joke. I took my wife to Santa Fe to see a doctor, but it was too late. She was a Mexican girl and her folks live there. They wanted her buried near her own people."

"Sorry," Jim Benton said, trying to hide a frown. Why did people tell him their troubles? He had no pity left to give.

"It was her idea to take the wagon and bring back a load of supplies," the man added, "and the girls wanted to go along, so we had to close our store in Rustler's Roost. That's why we're in a hurry to get back."

Benton took a closer look at the girls. Both had dark hair and eyes, but one had a smooth white face and the other's face was as brown as that of an Indian girl. Benton would never have guessed that she was half white, nor would he have been certain that the other girl was half Mexican. Both appeared to be around eighteen or nineteen. He had no idea which one was older.

"I'm Charlie Fry," the man said. "These are my girls, Rita and Nita." He grinned. "They ain't quite twins, but they only missed it by eleven months."

"Jim Benton," Benton said. He thought it unlikely that anyone in this area had heard of him.

It was obvious that Rita and Nita Fry had not, and just as obvious that they had no wish to get acquainted. The one with the clear white skin, whom he took to be Rita, gave him a cool glance. The other one did not even bother to glance at him.

Jim Benton touched the brim of his black hat and said dryly, "Nice meeting you." Then he touched the brown horse with his spurs and rode on along the trail.

"Maybe we'll see you in town," Charlie Fry called after him. "We should have the store open for business by tomorrow."

Benton rode on without replying or looking back.

The trail soon led him down out of the tall pines and wound among rocky hills dotted with stunted cedars. Below stretched the gray desert, and in the distance he caught a glimpse of a huddle of buildings that he took to be Rustler's Roost.

It was noon when he reached the one-street town. Most of the buildings were frame or log shacks with false fronts but here and there crouched a low-roofed adobe. The biggest adobe building said "FRY'S STORE" across the front. Riding past, Benton noticed the closed sign in the window.

Benton left his horse at the livery stable and walked back along the nearly deserted street with his saddlebags and blanket roll, turning into the two-story frame hotel, the Cedar House. It was the only hotel in town. He signed the register and paid a dollar for the first night. Going up to his room on the second floor, he dropped his saddlebags and blanket roll on the floor and glanced at the tall bleak-eyed stranger in the mirror, which showed him reversed, the holstered revolver on the left side.

Removing his hat and short close-fitting Mexican jacket, he rolled up his shirt sleeves, poured water from the pitcher into the basin on the wash-stand and washed his face and hands, drying with a towel. The clerk had told him that dinner was being served in the dining room. Going back down the stairs, he entered the dining room and ate at a table by himself in the corner, his back to the wall, ignoring the other diners who watched him with covert interest.

In the barbershop later, he got a shave and a hair trim and soaked a while in the barber's tub in the back room, then put on the clean clothes he had brought with him. They looked just like the clothes he had taken off, which he left at a Chinese laundry on his way back to the hotel.

In his room, he hung his hat and gun belt on the back of a chair and stretched out on the bed with his hands clasped behind his head, staring at the ceiling with still gray eyes.

He found himself thinking about the two girls he had seen on the wagon, Rita and Nita Fry. Rita's smooth white face had a rare, flawless beauty. But the other girl, though not quite as pretty, appeared to have a better figure, though not by much. They were both fine-looking girls, and all too well aware of it, Benton thought. From their quiet reserve and superior in-difference he would never have guessed that they were the daughters of a friendly and talkative man like Charlie Fry. They did not resemble him in any way either.

Benton was tired from long riding and after a while he fell asleep. He was awakened late in the day by the sound of yells, hoofbeats and gunshots. Rising, he went to the window to look out.

Four or five riders were galloping their horses back and forth along the dusty street, whooping and firing their pistols into the air. A bunch of wild young cowhands letting off steam, he decided.

But Benton's attention was drawn to an older man, a big man pushing forty with a strong weathered face and graying hair, who seemed to be with the others but taking no part in the fun. He quietly rode his horse to a saloon across the street, swung down rather stiffly, tied the animal and pushed in through the swing doors.

When the others tired of their sport they also headed for the saloon, laughing as they went in and slapping one another on the back.

Jim Benton's eyes were uneasy as he turned away from the window. It was usually the wild young ones like that who caused him trouble. Older men like that big quiet fellow had learned that it was better to avoid trouble. But some never learned. Some did not live long enough.

Benton thoughtfully buckled on his cartridge belt, drew the gun from the holster and checked it. The gun was a .44 Frontier Colt with a five-and-a-half inch barrel and a plain walnut butt. Benton did not wear the gun for show.

Slipping the gun back into the holster, he put on his black hat and a dark gray wool coat that was warmer than his thin charro jacket. Also, he did not want to be mistaken for a Mexican or a Mexican lover. This was evidently a gringo town and there was no point in asking for trouble.

As he went down the stairs he again thought of Rita and Nita Fry. He doubted if girls as pretty as those two would be rejected because they were part Mexican, especially in a country where there were so few girls of any kind.

They did not start serving supper in the dining room until six, so Benton left the hotel and crossed to a restaurant. There was no one in sight, but he heard someone moving around in back. He sat down at a table against the wall where he could see the door and the street through the window.

It was several minutes before a tired-looking slender woman of about thirty came from the kitchen and looked at him curiously. "Hello," she said. "What would you like?"

"Anything you've got to eat and some black coffee."

"Beef stew and potatoes sound all right?"

"Sounds fine."

She went back into the kitchen.

A moment later the street door opened and three young men in their twenties came in. They were three of the ones Benton had seen a little earlier galloping their horses up and down the street and firing their guns in the air. They stared at him now with eyes that were half friendly and half challenging. But they went on to the counter and took stools without speaking to him.

The woman returned from the kitchen with Benton's supper and one of the men at the counter drawled, "Hello, Mary. That for me?"

She smiled. "No, but I can bring you some more for fifty cents."

"Sounds like my credit ain't good here no more."

"Not till you boys pay what you owe me."

"How much is that?"

"A little over thirty dollars. I've got it written down in back."

"Thirty dollars! That much?"

"Yep." She set Benton's food on the table before him and went back around behind the counter, studying the three young men. "If just one of you would work for a month, you'd have enough to pay your bill here."

All three of them chuckled at the notion of working for a month just to pay what they owed her. The tall shaggy-haired rider who had spoken before said, "We got our own place to keep up, Mary."

"But you're not keeping it up," she said in the same tired but patient tone as before. "If you're not in town you're off causing devilment somewhere else. You haven't got any stock and you haven't even fixed up that old shack you boys moved into."

"Who told you all that, Mary?"

"You think there are any secrets in a place like this?" she asked. "Everybody in the country knows about you boys, and they're keeping their eyes on you, waiting for you to get caught. I believe they named the town in your honor. It didn't have a name for a long time."

"Thanks for the warning," the talker drawled, while the other two chuckled. "I'll remember you said that when they put a rope around our necks. But right now I'm more worried about my belly. Couldn't you feed us just one more time, Mary? We'll pay you the next time we get any money."

"You said that the last time. And the time before that. I'd keep feeding you boys on credit if I could, but I can't. If business doesn't pick up, it looks like I may have to close the restaurant."

"I'd sure hate for you to do that, Mary. This is the only restaurant in town, and they won't give us no credit at the hotel."

One of the others, a heavyset young man with a swarthy round face, turned on his stool and regarded Benton with narrow eyes. "This stranger looks like he's rollin' in dough. He shouldn't mind loanin' us five or ten bucks."

Benton kept his attention on his food. "Sorry."

"What does that mean?"

"I don't imagine I'll be around when you get the money to pay me back."

The chunky man scowled. "What's five or ten bucks?"

"About a week's pay for a cowhand," Benton said. "If you need money you might consider going to work, like the lady suggested."

The third man swung around angrily. He was almost as tall as the shaggy-haired rider and almost as dark as the short one. He had slightly rounded shoulders, a hooked nose and bright piercing eyes. "We don't need no suggestions from you, mister," he said.

"No, all you need is my money," Benton said dryly.

Both the hook-nosed rider and the chunky one started to get to their feet, their fists clenched.

"Take it easy, Hawk," the shaggy-haired rider said in an uneasy tone. "You too, Chunk."

"I ain't in no mood for no lip from no fancy dude," Hawk said, but he sat back down. So did Chunk, after scowling at Benton in silence for a moment.

"I don't want any trouble here," the woman said. "I guess I'll feed you boys this time, but it will have to be the last time till you pay me. I've been getting supplies on credit at Fry's Store, but I hate to keep asking him for more credit till I pay my bill. And he lost his wife. That doctor in Santa Fe couldn't do anything for her. They got back a little while ago and stopped here to eat so the girls wouldn't have to cook."

The shaggy-haired rider grinned. "You mean they're back already? We'll have to mosey over after supper and see how Rita and Nita are doin'."

"Charlie said he wasn't going to open the store until tomorrow. But you might give them a hand unloading the supplies they brought back, if they haven't finished already."

The rider chuckled. "Looks like you aim to put us to work one way or another, don't it?"

"You boys should all go to work and settle down, before you get in bad trouble," she said. "But I don't guess it would be too easy to find a job now. All the ranches are laying men off for the winter, instead of hiring more."

She went into the kitchen, and Hawk grunted, "Who the hell wants a job?" He remembered Benton and turned to glare at him. "What do you work at?"

"I'm between jobs at the moment."

Hawk's sharp eyes pushed at him. "What sort of jobs?"

The shaggy-haired rider said without turning, "Take it easy, Hawk."

Hawk's face contorted with anger. "Don't tell me what to do, Pete. You ain't my boss. If I wanted a damned boss, I'd go to work."

"No, you wouldn't," Pete said. "You'd do anything to keep from goin' to work, just like me."

The chunky rider chuckled, and Hawk relaxed, turning as the woman came back with a plate of food in each hand.

"How much do I owe you, ma'am?" Benton asked.

"Fifty cents."

He laid a dollar on the table and rose.

"Wait," she said, "and I'll get your change."

"Forget it." He glanced at the three men sitting at the counter. "Just don't let anybody steal it."

Then he went out.

The preceding was from the gritty western novel
The Hellbound Man

To keep reading, click or go here:
http://amzn.to/1fTATJy

Excerpt from
Rebel With A Gun
by Van Holt

On a gray, drizzly day in the spring of 1865, a tall slender young man on a brown horse rode along the muddy street of Hayville, Missouri. Several heads turned to stare at him, but he seemed not to notice anyone, and he did not stop in the town, but rode on out to a weather-beaten, deserted-looking house and dismounted in the weed-grown yard.

At the edge of the yard there was a grave surrounded by a low picket fence and he went that way and stood with his head bared in the slow drizzle and stared at the grave with bleak, bitter blue eyes. He was only nineteen but looked thirty. He had been only fifteen when the war started. That seemed like a lifetime ago, another world —a world that had been destroyed. All that was left was a deserted battlefield, a devastated wasteland swarming with scavengers and pillagers.

An old black man with only one eye appeared from a dripping pine thicket and slowly reached up to remove a battered hat and scratch the white fuzz on his head.

"Dat you, Mistuh Ben?"

"It's me, Mose," Ben Tatum said.

"I knowed sooner or later you'd come back to see yo' ma's grave. She died two years back now. Never was the same aftuh we heard the news about yo' pa. And too she was worried sick about you. Is it true you rode with Quantrill, Mistuh Ben?"

"You can hear anything, Mose."

"Yessuh, dat's de truth, it sho' is. But I wouldn't rightly blame you if you did. Dem Yankees sho' did raise hell, didn't they, Mistuh Ben?"

Old Mose was something of a diplomat. Had he been talking to a Yankee, he would have said it was the Rebels who had raised hell.

Or he might have said it was Quantrill's raiders.

"The war's over, Mose."

"Yessuh, I sho' do hope so, I sho' do." Old Mose reached up and rubbed his good eye, and for a moment his blind eye seemed to peer at the tall young man in the old coat. "But folks say there's some who still ain't surrendered and don't plan to. I hear there ain't no amnesty for Quantrill's men. Is dat true, Mistuh Ben?"

"That's what I heard, Mose."

"Dat sho' is too bad. I guess dat mean there still be ridin' and shootin' and burnin' just like befo'."

"Maybe not, Mose."

"I sho' do hope not. Has you only got one gun, Mistuh Ben? I hear some of Quantrill's men carry fo' or five all at one time."

Ben Tatum glanced down at the double-action Cooper Navy revolver in his waistband. He buttoned his coat over the gun. "I just got in the habit of carrying this one, Mose. I wouldn't feel right without it."

"Guess a man can't be too careful dese days." Old Mose thoughtfully rubbed the wide bridge of his nose, his good eye wandering off down the road toward Hayville. "Well, I just come by to check on yo' ma's grave. She sho' was a fine woman. Mistuh Snyder down to de bank own de place now. I guess you heard his boy Cal done gone and married dat Farmer girl you was sweet on?"

Ben Tatum let out a long sigh. "No, I hadn't heard, Mose. But it doesn't matter now. I can't stay here."

Old Mose looked like he had lost his only friend. "Where will you go, Mistuh Ben?"

"I don't know yet. West, maybe."

He turned and looked at the old house with its warped shingles and staring, broken windows. He did not go inside. He knew the house would be as empty as he felt.

He turned toward his horse.

"Oh, Mistuh Ben!"

"What is it, Mose?"

"I almost forgot," old Mose said, limping forward. "Yo' ma's sister, what live over to Alder Creek, she said if I ever saw you again to be sho' and tell you to come by and see her."

"All right, Mose. Thanks."

He thoughtfully reached into a pocket, found a coin and tossed it to the old Negro.

A gnarled black hand shot up and plucked the coin out of the air. "Thanks, Mistuh Ben. I sho' do 'preciate it. Times sho' is hard since they went and freed us darkies. Them Yankees freed us but they don't feed us."

He rode back through Hayville. The small town seemed all but deserted. But it had always seemed deserted on rainy days, and sometimes even on sunny days. But for some reason Ben Tatum could no longer recall very many sunny days. They had faded into the mist of time, the dark horror of war.

He stopped at a store to get a few supplies. The sad-eyed old man behind the counter seemed not to recognize him. But Ben Tatum had been only a boy when he had left, and now he was a tall young man with shaggy brown hair and a short beard. He had not shaved on purpose because he had no wish to be recognized. And he suspected that old man Hill did not recognize him on purpose. It was usually best not to recognize men who had ridden with Quantrill.

The slow rain had stopped, and when he left the store Ben Tatum saw a few people stirring about. A handsome, well-dressed young couple were going along the opposite walk. The young man had wavy dark hair and long sideburns, a neatly trimmed mustache. He wore a dark suit and carried a cane, like a dandy, and his arrogant face was familiar. The girl had long dark hair and just a hint of freckles. It was Jane Farmer. Only it would be Jane Snyder now. Cal Snyder had stayed here and courted her and married her while Ben Tatum was dodging bullets and sleeping out in the wet and cold, when he got a chance to sleep at all. Cal Snyder had not gone to the war. His father had hired a man to go in his place, a man who had not come back. He had been killed at Shiloh.

Ben Tatum stopped and stared at her as if a mule had kicked him in the belly. But neither Jane Snyder nor her dandified husband showed the slightest sign that they recognized him or even saw him. They went on along the walk and turned into the restaurant.

With a sick hollow feeling inside him, Ben Tatum got back in his wet saddle and rode on along the muddy street, returning to the bleak empty world from which he had come, homeless now and a wanderer forever. The war had taught him how to lose. Turn your back and ride off as if it did not matter. Never let the winners know you cared.

"Ben! Ben Tatum!"

For a fleeting moment hope rose up in him like an old dream returning. But then he realized that it was not her voice, and when he looked around he saw a fresh-faced girl just blooming into womanhood, a girl with long light brown hair that was almost yellow and a face that looked somehow familiar. She was smiling and radiant and seemed happy to see him. Puzzled, he searched his memory but failed to place her, and it made him uneasy. He lived in a world where it did not pay to trust your closest friends, much less strange beautiful girls who seemed too happy to see you. Many girls that age had been spies during the war and had lured many a dazzled man to their destruction. Some of them might still be luring men to their destruction, for the war still was not over for some men and never would be over. Men like Ben Tatum. And the fact that she knew his name proved nothing.

So he merely touched his hat and kept his horse at the same weary trot along the muddy street, and behind him he heard a little exclamation: "Well!" He rode on out of town, wondering who she was. He noticed that it had started raining again.

Alder Creek was a two-day ride west of Hayville. There were no streets in Alder Creek, just narrow roads that wound among the trees that grew everywhere, and most of the houses were scattered about in clearings that had been hacked out of the trees and brush.

Ben Tatum's aunt lived in a big old house on a shelf above the hidden murmuring creek that had given the town its name. Her husband had died years ago in a mysterious hunting accident and she had soon remarried and had a lively stepdaughter. Her two sons had died in the war and she had no other children of her own.

Cora Wilburn had been a slender, attractive woman in her late thirties the last time Ben Tatum had seen her. But the war had aged her as it had aged everyone else. There were lines in her tired face and streaks of gray in her hair, and she had put on weight. But she seemed glad to see him, and it was good to see a smiling, friendly face.

She hugged him and patted his back just the way his own mother would have done had she lived to see him come home. "My, you've sure grown into a tall, fine-looking man," she said, blinking away tears. Her voice sounded as old and tired as she looked. "But you need a haircut and some decent clothes. Sam's a pretty good barber, they tell me, and you can have some of

Dave's clothes. He was tall like you. I appreciate the nice letter you sent me when Dave and Lot were killed."

He nodded, and just then he noticed a tall slender girl of about thirteen standing on the porch watching him with lively green eyes and a mischievous smile. "This can't be Kittie," he said in a slow surprise.

"Yes, that's Kittie," Cora Wilburn said in her tired voice. "Ain't she run up like a weed? Soon be grown. It's getting hard to keep the boys away from her or her away from the boys."

Kittie Wilburn gave her dark head a little toss and flashed her white teeth in a smile, but said nothing.

"Sam's at the barbershop," Cora Wilburn added. "Soon as you eat a bite and catch your breath, you should go on down there and get some of that hair cut off your head and face. I want to see what you look like without that beard."

Sam Wilburn was a strange, moody man, by turns silent and talkative. He had a habit of watching you out of the corners of cold green eyes, without ever facing you directly. He was trimming an old man's white hair when Ben Tatum opened the door of the small barbershop. He glanced up at him out of those strange green eyes and said, "Have a seat. I'll be with you in a few minutes."

Ben Tatum sat down in a chair against the wall and picked up an old newspaper. The war was still going on when the newspaper was printed, but Quantrill had already disappeared and was thought dead by them and his followers had scattered, some of them forming small guerrilla bands of their own, or degenerating into common outlaws and looters, preying on the South as well as the North. Others had gone into hiding or left the country. Few had any homes left to return to, even if it had been safe to go home.

When the old man left, Ben Tatum took his place in the barber's chair and Sam Wilburn went to work on his hair. He did not seem very happy to see the younger man. They had never had much use for each other, and now and then Ben Tatum had idly wondered if Sam Wilburn had arranged the hunting accident that had left Cora Medlow an attractive young widow. Why Cora had married Sam Wilburn was another mystery he still had not figured out. But the world was full of things he would probably never understand.

Sam Wilburn glanced through the window at a wagon creaking down the crooked, stump-dotted road that passed for the town's main street. "I've been wondering when you'd show up," he said. When Ben Tatum made no reply, he asked, "You been to the house?"

Ben Tatum grunted in the affirmative.

Sam Wilburn worked in silence for a time, evidently doing a thorough job of it. The coarse brown hair fell on the apron in chunk's. Scattered among the brown, there were hairs that looked like copper wires, and there were more of them in his beard, especially on his chin. Those dark reddish copper hairs gleamed in his hair and short beard.

"What do you plan to do, now that the war's over?" Wilburn asked, his attention on his work.

"I ain't decided yet."

"You can't stay around here. They'll be looking for you."

Ben Tatum sighed, but said nothing. He sighed because he knew Sam Wilburn did not want him to stay around here. He had known already that they would be looking for him.

"Texas," Sam Wilburn said. "That's your best bet. I've been thinking about going down there myself. I don't think I'll like it much around here when the carpetbaggers move in. I don't like nobody telling me what to do or how to run my business."

"I doubt if it will be much better in Texas."

"Can't be any worse. Quite a few others around here and Hayville feel the same way. They've been talking about getting up a whole wagon train and going down there."

"I imagine talk about it is about all they'll ever do."

"No, they're serious. Even old Gip Snyder is talking about going. He says it's a new country with a lot of opportunities and we can build ourselves a new town down there where nobody won't bother us. Course, he plans to start a new bank, and I could start a new barbershop. The more I think about it, the better I like the idea."

"There'll be carpetbaggers in Texas just like there are here," Ben Tatum said.

"It won't be as bad. This state's been torn apart worse by the war than any other state in the country, and now that it's safe the carpetbaggers will be flocking in like vultures to pick our bones. Our money's already worthless. That's why old Gip Snyder is so keen on going. His bank at Hayville is in trouble, and he wants to salvage what he can and get out."

Ben Tatum shifted uncomfortably in the chair. "What about all the property he owns around Hayville?"

"I think he's found a buyer for most of it. That's the only thing that worries me. I don't know what I'd do with our property here if I went, and Cora ain't too keen on going. She's been in bad health lately. Losing them boys nearly killed her."

Ben Tatum was silent.

After a moment Wilburn asked, "What about the beard?"

"Get rid of it, I guess. Aunt Cora don't seem to like it."

After supper Ben Tatum went for a walk down along the creek. A path led him past an old shack almost hidden in the trees and brush. There was a light burning in the shack and through the window he caught a glimpse of a very shapely, blond-haired woman taking a bath. The long hair looked familiar.

When he got back to the Wilburn house he found Kittie in his room. "What are you doing here?" he asked, taking off the coat Aunt Cora had given him. It had belonged to Dave Medlow but it fitted Ben Tatum all right.

Kittie's lips curled back from her white teeth in a teasing smile. "Straightening up your room, Cousin Ben," she said with a deliberately exaggerated southern drawl.

"You run along," he said. "I'm not your cousin and the room don't need straightening up."

"That's right, we ain't cousins, are we?" she said. "We ain't no kin a'tall, now I think about it. But I was gonna marry you anyway. You sure do look handsome without that old beard. It made you look like a old man of about thirty."

"I'll be thirty before you're dry behind the ears," he said. He hung the coat in the closet and put his gun in a bureau drawer. In the mirror he saw Kittie Wilburn watching him with a smile, and he turned around with a frown. "Are you still here?"

"No, I'm still leaving. I just ain't got very far yet." She lay down on the bed and put her bare feet up on the gray wallpaper, so that her skirt fell down around her thighs, revealing very shapely legs for a skinny, thirteen-year-old girl. "Did you go see Rose?" she asked.

"Who?"

"Rose Harper. That girl who lives down by the creek. She just got back from Hayville a little while ago. I saw her go by. She lives over here now. Ever since she married Joe Harper. But she don't stay here much, 'cause he ain't never around. The bluebellies and nearly everybody else is looking for him, 'cause he rode with Quantrill. Like you."

"What does she look like?"

"Don't you know? You went to see her, didn't you? Anyway, you used to know her when she lived at Hayville with her folks."

"Wait a minute," Ben Tatum said. "Didn't Joe Harper marry that Hickey girl? Rose Hickey?"

"He shore did, Cousin Ben. He shore did."

"I thought that was what he told me after he came home the last time.

My God, she was just a kid the last time I saw her."

"She ain't no kid now."

"She sure ain't," Ben Tatum agreed. "I saw her in Hayville and didn't even recognize her."

"I hate her," Kittie Wilburn said. "She makes me look plumb scrawny." She pulled her skirt up a little higher and looked at her thighs. "Do you think I'll ever outgrow it, Cousin Ben? Looking so scrawny and all?"

"You might," he said, "if I don't get mad and wring your neck."

"Oh, all right. I'll go." She swung her bare feet to the floor and rose, stretching and making a sort of groaning sound in her throat. She looked at him with that teasing smile. "But you've got to promise me something first."

"What?"

"I'll have to whisper it. I don't want anyone else to hear." She put her arms around his neck and rose on tiptoes, putting her warm moist lips close to his ear and whispering, "You've got to promise to marry me someday. Then I'll go."

"That'll be the day!"

She giggled and again made as if to whisper something, but this time she bit his ear and then ran from the room. At the door she pulled her skirt up to her waist, bent over and showed him her bottom. And it was quite a bottom for a skinny, thirteen-year-old girl to be flashing. He saw it in his mind until he went to sleep, and he wondered if he was the only one who had seen it. If so, it was probably only because she had not had an opportunity to show it to anyone else.

He knew he should tell Aunt Cora about the girl's naughty behavior, for her own good. But he also knew that he wouldn't, for his own good. Aunt Cora might think he had encouraged the child in some way, and think less of him because of it.

He slept late the next morning, and was awakened by the slamming of the door when Sam Wilburn left for the barbershop. He had just gotten dressed when he heard a dozen or more horsemen crowding into the yard, ordering all those inside to come out with their hands in the air.

The preceding was from the western novel
Rebel With A Gun

To keep reading, click or go here:
http://amzn.to/1apARDN

Excerpt from
Dead Man Riding
by Van Holt

Nine tough-looking men, most of them bearded and dirty, all heavily armed, were lined up at the plank bar that windy Saturday afternoon when the stranger rode into the small adobe town of Bandanna. They heard the sound of his horse walking quietly down the short dusty street and then the creak of leather as he dismounted in front of the saloon.

Sharp eyes turned or watched him in the back-bar window as he came in through the batwing doors. They saw a tall young man in his late twenties, with broad shoulders and a lean waist. His hair was brown and thick under the wide-brimmed, low-crowned hat; his eyes were gray and cold under frowning brows. His coat was unbuttoned and they saw that he wore two guns, one in a tied-down holster, the other thrust into his waistband with the walnut butt to the right for a cross draw.

A noticeable change came over the nine men already at the bar. They exchanged silent glances, or stared hard at the tall stranger. Dark eyes got darker, pale eyes seemed to freeze in their sockets.

He stopped at the front end of the bar, several feet from Dudley Haskett, and said one quiet word to the chunky bartender.

"Whiskey."

The bartender put a bottle and a glass on the plank bar and then went back to polishing glasses. The saloon was so quiet that the noise made by the stranger uncorking the bottle seemed loud in the silence. Outside the wind moaned like a lost soul in limbo, but there was no other sound.

Then, as the stranger slowly sipped his whiskey, Haskett's dark beard parted in a white-toothed grin and he said, "You lookin' for work, stranger?"

The stranger glanced at him in surprise. The other men at the bar seemed equally surprised.

"Hadn't thought about it."

"I'm Dudley Haskett, foreman of the Spradlin ranch. You must of heard of Hoot Spradlin?"

"Can't say as I have."

Haskett's grin faded, to be replaced by a look of astonishment. "Then you must not be from these parts."

"Nope."

Haskett hesitated. "Mind if I ask yore name?"

"Frank Stanton."

There was a little intake of breath along the bar, a sudden tensing of gun hands.

Dudley Haskett leaned slightly toward him. "You mind sayin' that again?"

The stranger, still holding the glass in his left hand, repeated the name in the same quiet tone.

Haskett relaxed a little and his grin returned, but he continued to study the stranger closely. "There for a minute I thought you said Fanton. You wouldn't happen to know a man by that name, would you?"

"Fanton?" The stranger seemed to think for a moment, then shook his head. "No, I don't think so."

Haskett wiped his palms on his trousers, his eyes haunted. "Well, we were about to head back for the ranch. Be supper time 'fore we get there, and there don't seem to be much doin' in town. If you want to ride along, I'll speak to the boss about givin' you a job. But you might get stuck in a shack by yoreself or with just one other man, ridin' line. Ain't much else to do in the winter."

Stanton finished his drink. "I don't mind riding line."

Haskett's grin was uneasy. "Somehow I didn't figger you would."

They left money on the plank bar and filed outside. The hard-eyed Spradlin men watched Stanton mount his roan gelding. Then they silently untied their own horses and mounted up. Haskett and Stanton took the lead as they rode away from the bleak huddle of earth-colored buildings that was usually just called town. It was hardly ever called Bandanna.

Stanton glanced back once, then turned his gray eyes to the brush-spotted plains ahead. "The Spradlin ranch a pretty big outfit?" he asked as if just making idle conversation.

Haskett grinned. "One of the biggest in southwest Texas." Then he added, "We're on it now, as a matter of fact. Ain't no other ranches around but a few squatters that Hoot has been talkin' about runnin' off."

Stanton fell silent, his eyes strangely bleak and bitter under his wide hatbrim.

The ranch headquarters turned out to be a half-dugout sticking out of the side of a barren rocky hill dotted with dwarf cedars, a low adobe bunkhouse and cookshack adjoining, some sheds and a tangle of pole corrals. There was a spring nearby and a lonely old cottonwood tree whose bare branches rattled in the cold wind.

It was almost dark when the ten men arrived, but Stanton saw the rope dangling from the lowest limb of the cottonwood. There was an empty noose at the end of the rope and the rope swung in the wind.

"That's where we hung Fanton," Haskett said, watching him closely as they rode by the tree.

For a moment Stanton's hand went to his neck, but he said nothing.

The bunkhouse was dark, but lamplight showed at the cookshack and the half-dugout. The ten men dismounted at the corrals, and Haskett said, "One of you boys take care of Stanton's horse. Me and him will go in to see Hoot about that job."

Haskett and the tall silent stranger crossed to the half-dugout and passed in under a brush-roofed unfloored porch to enter a large long room that contained a combination bar and store counter at the front and living quarters at the back.

Two slender, attractive blond-haired women, one in her late thirties, the other a girl of about nineteen, were quietly eating supper at a plank table in the back. The girl, very pretty despite a pouting mouth and unhappy eyes, looked at Stanton with no hint of a smile. The older woman did not even glance in his direction, though she sat facing the door.

Behind the counter stood a lean dark man of about fifty. His eyes were black and malevolent, one much smaller than the other.

Haskett touched his hat to the two women at the back and then spoke to the dark man. "Got a man here lookin' for work, Hoot." There was a little pause before he added, "Says his name's Frank Stanton."

Hoot Spradlin's bigger eye widened in surprise, the other became a gleaming black slit. For a long moment he peered at Stanton in the dim lamplight, and what he saw did not lessen the suspicion and hatred in his eyes.

"Might be you wouldn't like it here," he said finally. "We have a lot of trouble with Comanches and white rustlers, not to mention greasers from across the border. We just buried two men. That's the only reason I'd be interested in hirin' you."

Stanton shrugged his broad shoulders. "That's about what I expected."

Hoot Spradlin stared at him a moment in silence, then reluctantly nodded. "Go to the bunkhouse and find yourself a bunk. And you better get on over to the cookshack or there won't be nothin' left."

Stanton silently nodded and turned to leave.

"You stay here a minute, Dudley," Spradlin said. "Somethin' I want to ask you."

Stanton paused outside in the gathering darkness and looked toward the cottonwood where the noose swung in the wind.

Behind him in the half-dugout he heard Spradlin say, "You sure he didn't say his name was Fanton?"

"No, he said Stanton. I asked him twice just to make shore."

"Looks a lot like Fanton, don't he?"

"Shore does. That's the main reason I brought him out here. I figgered you'd want a look at him."

"Keep a eye on him and try to find out who he is and what he's doin' here," Spradlin said. "And tell the hands to watch him."

"They been watchin' him like he was a ghost. I almost believe he is, my own self."

The preceding was from the gritty western novel

Dead Man Riding

To keep reading, click or go here:
http://amzn.to/1aknrFD

More hellbound gunslinging westerns by Van Holt:

A Few Dead Men
http://amzn.to/18Xu7ic

Blood in the Hills
http://amzn.to/16jWNvB

Brandon's Law
http://amzn.to/1fijGsy

Curly Bill and Ringo
http://amzn.to/Z6AhSH

Dead Man Riding
http://amzn.to/1aknrFD

Dead Man's Trail
http://amzn.to/ZcPJ47

Death in Black Holsters
http://amzn.to/1aHxGcv

Dynamite Riders
http://amzn.to/ZyhHmg

Hellbound Express
http://amzn.to/11i3NcY

Hunt the Killers Down
http://amzn.to/Z7UHjD

Maben
http://amzn.to/1judfzK

Rebel With A Gun
Coming Soon!

Riding for Revenge
http://amzn.to/13gLILz

Rubeck's Raiders
http://amzn.to/14CDxwU

Shiloh Stark
http://amzn.to/12ZJxcV

Shoot to Kill
http://amzn.to/18zA1qm

Six-Gun Solution
http://amzn.to/10t3H3N

Six-Gun Serenade

http://amzn.to/164cS7t

Son of a Gunfighter
http://amzn.to/17QAzSp

The Antrim Guns
http://amzn.to/132I7jr

The Bounty Hunters
http://amzn.to/10gJQ6C

The Bushwhackers
http://amzn.to/13ln4JO

The Fortune Hunters
http://amzn.to/11i3VsO

The Gundowners
(formerly So, Long Stranger)
http://amzn.to/16c0I2J

The Gundown Trail
http://amzn.to/1g1jDNs

The Hellbound Man
http://amzn.to/1fTATJy

The Last of the Fighting Farrells
http://amzn.to/Z6AyVI

The Long Trail
http://amzn.to/137P9c8

The Man Called Bowdry
http://amzn.to/14LjpJa

The Return of Frank Graben
Coming Soon!

The Revenge of Sam Graben
Coming Soon!

The Stranger From Hell
http://amzn.to/12qVVqd

The Vultures
http://amzn.to/12bjeGl

Wild Country
http://amzn.to/147xUDq

Wild Desert Rose
http://amzn.to/XH7Y27

Brought to you by Three Knolls Publishing
Independent Publishing in the Digital Age

www.3knollspub.com

About the Author:

Van Holt wrote his first western when he was in high school and sent it to a literary agent, who soon returned it, saying it was too long but he would try to sell it if Holt would cut out 16,000 words. Young Holt couldn't bear to cut out any of his perfect western, so he threw it away and started writing another one.

A draft notice interrupted his plans to become the next Zane Grey or Louis L'Amour. A tour of duty as an MP stationed in South Korea was pretty much the usual MP stuff except for the time he nabbed a North Korean spy and had to talk the dimwitted desk sergeant out of letting the guy go. A briefcase stuffed with drawings of U.S. aircraft and the like only caused the overstuffed lifer behind the counter to rub his fat face, blink his bewildered eyes, and start eating a big candy bar to console himself. Imagine Van Holt's surprise a few days later when he heard that same dumb sergeant telling a group of new admirers how he himself had caught the famous spy one day when he was on his way to the mess hall.

Holt says there hasn't been too much excitement since he got out of the army, unless you count the time he was attacked by two mean young punks and shot one of them in the big toe. Holt believes what we need is punk control, not gun control.

After traveling all over the West and Southwest in an aging Pontiac, Van Holt got tired of traveling the day he rolled into Tucson and he has been there ever since, still dreaming of becoming the next Zane Grey or Louis L'Amour when he grows up. Or maybe the next great mystery writer. He likes to write mysteries when he's not too busy writing westerns or eating Twinkies.

WARNING: Reading a Van Holt western may make you want to get on a horse and hunt some bad guys down in the Old West. Of course, the easiest and most enjoyable way to do it is vicariously – by reading another Van Holt western.

Van Holt writes westerns the way they were meant to be written.

Printed in Great Britain
by Amazon.co.uk, Ltd.,
Marston Gate.